DALAL'S STREET

ANURAG TRIPATHI

olive turtle

NIYOGI BOOKS

Published by
NIYOGI BOOKS
Block D, Building No. 77,
Okhla Industrial Area, Phase-I,
New Delhi-110 020, INDIA
Tel: 91-11-26816301, 26818960
Email: niyogibooks@gmail.com
Website: www.niyogibooksindia.com

Editor: Mohua Mitra
Layout: Shraboni Roy
Cover design: Misha Oberoi

ISBN: 978-93-89136-15-9
Publication: 2019

Printed at: Niyogi Offset Pvt. Ltd., New Delhi, India

To my mother, who taught me that humility was not a sign of weakness, that giving didn't make me poorer, and without whom I would have been a lesser person...

A SLIPPERY SLOPE

Risk Taker to Naysayer

Thursday, the 23rd of April, 1992 started like any other day. On his way to office, Mr Aggarwal purchased a copy of the morning paper from his neighbourhood vendor. On the bus, he read the huge headlines, 'The Big Bull Caught in Crosshairs', announcing the stock market scam by the biggest bull of Dalal Street, Harshad Mehta. Mr Aggarwal was a committed investor, but didn't pay much heed to the article. Scams were common, they had happened before and would continue to occur in the future. The results were always the same: the big guys were seldom convicted. He was convinced that it wouldn't be any different this time. There would be the usual hullabaloo for a few days and then it would be business as usual. The 'Big Bull' was too damn big to be tamed by the newspaper article. He marked a few stocks in the paper and hoped that the prices of shares would correct sharply and fall. Perhaps it was an opportunity to buy.

As he got off the bus and walked towards his office, he was surprised to see a huge crowd assembled outside the building. Curious, he pushed through the onlookers. He could just make out the outline of a man's lifeless body lying in the middle of the road. There was no shattered glass or vehicle in the vicinity. This was no case of accident; the poor soul must have committed suicide, he thought. As he moved closer to the body, the contours of the face became familiar, he froze midstep and his legs gave way.

In front of him, in a big pool of blood, lay the body of his boss, the chairman of his bank. He was a kind, hearty man, respected by all members of the banking community. What had driven such a good, powerful man to commit suicide?

The Harshad Mehta scam, as it would come to be known, had just claimed its first life.

Shocked and panic stricken, Mr Aggarwal made his way into the office. The enormity of the scam slowly dawned on him and his life appeared to be crumbling before his eyes. All his life's savings were invested in the stocks recommended by the big bull. After all, he had received tips directly from the horse's mouth. Harshad Mehta was a regular at his bank. There was excitement every time he visited in his shining imported cars. He was generous in his stock tips and he gave them frequently, much to the delight of the bank employees. He was the Amitabh Bachchan of the stock markets who 'didn't create waves but rode on them.' Mehta had been photographed only a month earlier feeding peanuts to the bears at the Mumbai Zoo, a reflection of his victory over the bear cartel on Dalal Street.

How could it have gone so wrong?

Varun had distinct memories of that day and they always evoked mixed emotions. Children from the neighbourhood had gathered at his house to celebrate his fourth birthday. There was a lot of noise and excitement. The pineapple cake looked fresh and delicious, ready to be devoured. Everyone waited anxiously for his father, Mr Aggarwal, to return from work.

But the clock ticked away and minutes became hours; the noise and excitement died down. Soon, the children became restless and began leaving for their homes. Mrs Aggarwal, who had also been waiting for her husband and had uneasily watched the children get impatient, decided to salvage whatever was left of the situation. She asked her son to cut the cake. But Varun refused. He would not cut it until his father was there to clap and sing. Another half an hour passed by, the guests all left without eating the cake. The four-year-old birthday boy waited alone by the front door. By 10.30 pm he was exhausted and could no longer keep his eyes open.

It was midnight when Mr Aggarwal returned from office. He had had more than a few drinks and his footsteps were heavy and uneven.

He walked into his son's room. Varun was fast asleep. The moonlight fell on his face, highlighting the traces of tears across his cheeks.

Mr Aggarwal sat on the bed beside his son and mumbled an apology.

'Forgive me son,' he whispered. 'It hurts, but I couldn't be with you earlier today, I was too ashamed to look you in the eye. I didn't know what to do.'

He kissed Varun on the forehead and walked back to the living room. He didn't have the heart to confront his wife. What would he tell her? He had lost it all, gambled their entire life's savings on the stock markets. They would have to start all over again.

As he lay down on the couch alone that night, he made a promise to himself. Never again was he going to invest a rupee in the stock market. This incident had changed him forever. That morning he had been a risk taker who always read the pink papers looking for opportunities to invest; a few hours later, he had become a naysayer.

The cake was never cut.

He Didn't Have a Choice

Rajesh Reddy's palms were sweating and he bit his lips for the umpteenth time. He couldn't remember when he had felt like this. A first generation entrepreneur, he was the promoter of Reddy Oil & Gas, a company engaged in the business of oil exploration and drilling. Today, as he sat in the Presidential suite of the Taj Mahal hotel, he was clearly nervous. But then, he was not here by choice.

During the oil boom of 2007-8, when oil traded above the US$ 100 mark, Reddy had gone on a shopping spree, lapping up two of his competitors within a matter of six months, thereby becoming the largest player in the oil drilling sector in India.

Only one company had survived this ruthless blitzkrieg–Bansal Oil & Drilling. People speculated that it was Reddy himself who had blessed the Gargs of Bansal Oil & Drilling, allowing them to continue their operation. After all, it was essential to have a competitor, otherwise the regulator, The Competition Commission of India, would have been up in arms. But Reddy ensured that Bansal Oil & Drilling merely survived.

These acquisitions were made on the back of borrowings taken from banks whose chairmen were only too happy to fuel Reddy's rising ambition. After all, with oil moving up continuously to the US$ 140 mark, who could have guessed that the rigs operated by Reddy wouldn't be in demand in the foreseeable future?

The thriving business meant that Reddy Oil & Gas had become the darling of the stock markets, its share price reflecting the ambition of its promoter and hitting the *52-week high*, constantly. Trading at a price of Rs 600 per share, the company was valued at Rs 1200 crores.

In order to reduce his cost of borrowing, Reddy was advised to borrow in foreign currency. The Indian economy was on a strong footing and the risk of the Indian Rupee (Rs) weakening against the US$ was minimal. Foreign Currency Convertible Bonds (FCCB) were the flavour of the season. They were available to Reddy at an interest of 4 per cent payable in US$. This rate of interest was much lower than the 13 per cent that Reddy had to pay on his domestic borrowings from Indian banks. This would result in significant cost savings. Also, the bond holders had the option to convert their bonds into shares of Reddy Oil & Gas at the time of redemption. As per the terms negotiated by Reddy, the price for conversion of bonds into shares was set at Rs 450, while their own shares currently traded at Rs 600, i.e. at a significant premium to this conversion price. Reddy was confident that he wouldn't have to pay back a dime to the bond holders since it would be far more profitable for them to convert their bonds into shares of his company and enjoy the joyride with him, rather than ask for their capital to be returned. Accordingly, Reddy agreed to issue a FCCB of US$ 50 million, redeemable after seven years, i.e. in the year 2015.

But no one can predict the future. Shit hit the fan with the collapse of the Lehman Brothers and the global financial meltdown that followed, dragging companies and economies alike into recession. With global recession, oil prices crashed to a low of US$ 40 a barrel. With demand for oil expected to weaken in the foreseeable future, the exploration budget of the big oil companies was cut immediately. As a result, the rental market for oil rigs, which were the backbone of the oil exploration industry, also crashed.

Reddy got caught on the wrong side of trade, holding far more than he had bargained for. Intelligent business decisions, made only a few months earlier, didn't appear very smart in hindsight. On one hand, his acquisitions which were funded primarily by debt, resulted in his interest costs spiralling out of control; on the other, the dampened business environment ensured that most of his rigs remained out of business. It was a double whammy—increased costs and downturn in business.

With little to hold on to, Reddy turned to his friends at the banks. He had cultivated them for many years now, specifically for a day like this, throwing lavish parties where the glitterati of Bollywood entertained and divas danced with them on racy numbers. He had gifted them watches that they had only heard about and cars they had only dreamt of or read about in magazines. These people led a lifestyle predominantly funded by the likes of him. It was time to call in the favours.

They did save him eventually, not because of their friendship–he had to once again grease their palms with boxes full of cash–but because they were worried that if he went under, it might open a Pandora's Box that would take a few of them along with him. Everyone wanted to forget about the excesses allowed during the good times. Accordingly, loans were restructured. Not only was the average tenure period of his loans increased from three to five years, he was also provided with a moratorium. Thus, Reddy got a new lease of life.

Meanwhile, central banks across the world started printing hundreds of billions of dollars and pumping them back into the world economy to restart its growth drivers. With the banking system flush with funds and borrowing costs at historical lows, there was an immediate improvement in investor confidence and a lagged effect on client demand. Consequently, prices of oil also rebounded sharply. His oil rigs which were out of business all this time were suddenly back in demand.

From the brink of extinction, Reddy was once again on a roll. He had seen an entire business cycle play out in front of his eyes during the past four years. The experience had humbled him. He was worried about the future. What if it happened again? What if the economic cycle took a turn again for the worst? He had somehow managed to survive this time, thanks to the restructured loans and luck. Would he be able to do it again?

While the bankers made peace with him, restructuring his loans, the stock markets had been less forgiving. They hadn't forgotten how his stock had crashed post the Lehman crisis. Reddy Oil & Gas, which had once ruled at over Rs 600 during the good times, had fallen to two digits in the aftermath of the Lehman collapse. The business environment in the oil drilling sector had improved since then, but the stock markets were still jittery and in no hurry to put their faith into his company again. As a result, his company's share traded at a price of Rs 200, only a fraction of its previous high.

Also, ever since his company had opted for the restructuring of loans, the taps of liquidity had dried up for him. The FCCB that he had taken in 2008 was due for redemption in a little less than three years. With his stock trading at Rs 200, the bond holders would demand their money back. All this was in order, except that he didn't have the money to pay them back.

◈

Some well-wishers had advised him that there was one person who could help him out of his present dilemma. They called him Salil-bhai. No one knew his full name, but he came highly recommended. He had risen from the back lanes of Ahmedabad and was now the unchallenged king of Dalal Street, the Mecca of Indian stock markets. So, here he was, waiting uneasily for the man he hoped would somehow resolve his problem.

Reddy looked at his watch again. He had been waiting for over 10 minutes now. He took out his handkerchief and wiped his sweaty palms. He wanted to get over with this meeting and he wanted it fast.

It Only Happens in Fairy Tales

Varun was in the cafeteria with his friends, Anil and Pooja. It was mid-afternoon in the month of April. They were all final year students pursuing their MBA in a mid-level business school. The academic season had ended nearly a month ago and they were currently interviewing with prospective employers.

Luck had favoured Varun and Pooja, both of whom had got a job with a textile company. It wasn't the sexiest job in the world, but it was a job none the less. Anil, on the other hand, had been less fortunate and was still on the lookout.

They were discussing a placement talk which was scheduled to take place later that week.

'Have you guys heard about this company called TBB Limited?' asked Pooja.

Pooja was hardworking, conservative, righteous, spoke from her heart and believed in the goodness of mankind. She liked stories with a happy ending. In short, she exhibited all the virtues of a typical middle-class family.

'No idea,' replied Anil, shaking his head with an expression of disinterest on his face.

Anil seldom involved himself with worldly matters—he was a simple carefree soul, who spent most of his time on mundane chores like eating, sleeping and drinking. He was affable and had an inherent ability to befriend people. He was a *jugaadu*, a 'fixer' and seized every opportunity to get free food, drinks or sex.

'I don't know much else, but I do know that TBB stands for The Big Bull,' replied Varun, who was generally well informed.

'What kind of name is that?' asked Pooja.

'It is a stock broking company,' he replied.

'No one seems to have heard of them. And it says here that they will not be conducting interviews to select candidates. How else can you select a candidate, I wonder? They might as well be picking cattle from the village market.'

'Perhaps it is a reflection of what they think of our esteemed business school,' said Varun sarcastically.

'Yeah, the less said about that, the better,' added Anil.

'Hey, our college is not that bad, okay! We have learnt something, right? I hope this TBB's methods are not a reflection of what they think of us,' said Pooja. 'Why would anyone want to join a company that doesn't respect its employees?'

'Actually, they do have one criterion,' said Varun. 'You need to be a local resident with friends and family residing in the city.'

'I guess that counts you out, Anil. Aren't your parents based in Meerut?' asked Pooja.

'So what?' replied Anil. 'I have done my schooling and college in this city. I am as much a city boy as any one of you.'

'Frankly, all this sounds very shady to me,' retorted Pooja. 'In any case, stock broking is a very volatile business. What job security does it offer? I know that the textile job sounds boring, but at least our jobs are safe.'

'Oh Aunty! I don't even have a bloody job and you are talking about job security. Show some sympathy towards us lesser mortals,' scowled Anil.

On any other day, Anil would have got a mouthful from Pooja, who despised being called 'Aunty'. Luckily her attention was on Varun. She hoped that he would concur with her and accept the textile offer. She had plans for the two of them in the future, but for now, all she wanted was that they remain together.

Varun considered Pooja a good friend. She was sweet, trustworthy and caring. He knew that she had a crush on him, but he was not attracted to her. His desire lay elsewhere.

He was still mulling over his reply when Devika walked up to them, sending a sudden rush of blood between his legs. He had been eyeing her for almost two years. She was the complete package—perfect curves, attitude and brains. He often fantasised about the two of them together, but had never asked her out. He wasn't sure how she would respond to his advances, but he was certain that Pooja would be devastated. And that, for him, was a good enough reason to not pursue his desire, since he cared about Pooja's feelings.

'I am sorry, guys, but I couldn't help overhearing your conversation,' said Devika. 'I hope I am not intruding.'

'Not at all,' said Varun, adding invitingly. 'Join us.'

Pooja threw her hands in the air in disapproval. She strongly disliked Devika who was very feminine, smartly dressed and always calculated in her dealings. Pooja, on the other hand, was a tomboy—a pair of jeans and a t-shirt saw her through almost all occasions. Besides, the fact that Varun was overly accommodating when it came to Devika had not escaped her attention.

Devika coolly disregarded Pooja's gesture and sat next to Anil, who gladly moved aside to create space for her. He noticed the plate with a burger in her hand and suddenly looked alert.

'Devika, how come you are not eating your usual salad today?' he asked.

'The salad was sold out,' she replied disappointedly. 'The chef tells me that I am quite a trend setter, a lot of people have started eating salad now.'

'Ha-ha! A trend setter, my ass,' said Pooja sarcastically.

'I can see you had a salad for lunch, didn't you Pooja?' said Devika, with a sweet smile.

'So?'

'Nothing! Just saying.'

There was silence at the table as Devika slowly negotiated her way around the burger, removing the bun, cheese and mayonnaise, until all she was left with was the meat patty. With every passing second, the smile on Anil's face became wider in anticipation of what was to follow.

'Anil, would you like to help me finish this burger?' she asked.

'Sure! I thought you'd never ask.'

Before any more words could be exchanged, he grasped the bun, stuffed it with cheese, mayonnaise and fries and started munching away greedily. Now he was fully awake.

Devika, on the other hand, was still busy cutting the meat patty into small pieces which could be easily eaten with a fork.

She looked up at Varun and said, 'In today's world job security is a fallacy. All organisations are commercial, they employ you only so long as you can deliver, or else you are fired.'

Varun couldn't help but nod his concurrence to this statement, much to Pooja's annoyance.

Then she looked straight at Pooja and smiled, 'I agree with you that textile is a boring sector, it doesn't have the flamboyance associated with stock broking. But it may be like you, safe and predictable.'

Pooja looked around for something to throw at her face. Varun squeezed her hand, gesturing to her to calm down.

He said, 'Sometimes, steady and boring wins the race.'

Pooja was thrilled that he had come to her defence.

'Haaah! That only happens in fairy tales,' replied Devika. 'It is interesting how we are reading the same brief and arriving at such contrasting conclusions,' she said. 'When I see volatility, I think about opportunity. While you guys are worried that the organisation is small and unknown, I am excited, because small organisations are unstructured and offer exponential growth opportunities that are usually not available in their larger counterparts.'

'I fear that a high-pressure competitive environment will result in unhealthy competition, a bloodbath, where all is fair to achieve the desired goals,' said Varun.

'What's wrong with that?' Devika protested. 'All is fair in love and war. Survival of the fittest is the law of nature. Who are we to question it? The path to success is always the right path.'

'What do you think, Anil?' she asked.

Anil was still busy polishing off the last of the fries and spoke with his mouth full.

'I have no such dilemma, beggars can't be choosers,' he replied. 'Unlike you guys, I don't have a job. Volatile, unstructured or unhealthy competition, I don't care, I am going for it.'

'What do you think Varun?' she asked.

Varun was still mulling over the question. While a challenging unstructured environment excited him, for like Devika he was ambitious and a go-getter, he also knew his limitations. Unlike Devika, his upbringing was based on a very different value system. He had a conscience that would never allow him to trample on anyone else to achieve success.

However, since childhood he had been fascinated by the stock markets, despite the fact that his father was vehemently opposed to them. He had dreamt about the markets for long and could not let such an opportunity pass.

He knew that his father would be furious. But then, this wasn't the first time he was going against the wishes of his old man. The decision to join this particular business school had also been his, despite his father's reservation. He remembered being impressed by the full-page advertisement in the national daily showing a classroom full of well-dressed people with laptops. That image just stuck in his mind and he discounted every other aspect about the school, including the fact that its students seldom found jobs. In retrospect, it wasn't the best decision of his life. But then, it wasn't the worst either. He wondered how he would handle his father if he took the job.

'I think the stock broking industry offers better growth prospects,' he replied.

That was the hammer on the nail. All four of them decided to attend the placement talk. Pooja wasn't very convinced, but under no circumstances was she going to allow Devika to have Varun all to herself.

We Need a New Story

A wheatish complexion, a petit frame and a height of five feet five inches gave Salil-bhai an unassuming appearance. In a bank he would easily be mistaken for a peon or a lower division clerk.

However, it was when he started speaking that he immediately drew attention. It had nothing to do with his language skills. His English was at best very mediocre, reflecting his education in a Gujarati medium school. It was what he said, and the poise with which he said it, that made people look up and take notice. He exuded confidence, the kind that made every word he said believable, and he had examples to back everything he said.

Reddy rose from his seat as Salil-bhai entered the suite from the adjoining room. He was wearing a simple maroon silk shirt and black trousers. In his hands, he carried a few mobile phones with prepaid cards, which had been purchased under different names.

'Reddy sahib! Sorry for making you wait,' he said as they shook hands and sat down.

'I got late because Goel sahib was sitting in the adjoining room. He would just not leave. I had to eventually tell him, "You will have to excuse me sir, as I have another meeting." I still need to earn my livelihood, you see.'

The confidence with which he dropped the name implied that he was referring to none other than Gagan Goel, one of the biggest industrialists in the country.

Reddy sported a smile, no longer upset that he had to wait, but rather delighted that he was in such esteemed company.

'*Bolo* Reddy sahib, what can I do for you? Don't be embarrassed and hide facts, *khul ke bolo*. I am like your doctor, if you don't confide in me and tell me your problem, how can I help you?'

'The market is not giving due recognition to my company.'

'Why do you say that?' asked Salil-bhai.

'Even Bansal Oil & Drilling is trading at higher valuation than my company. The Gargs didn't even have the courage to look me in the eye, a few years back.'

'Don't rest on your laurels, Reddy sahib. The Gargs are doing extremely well, if their numbers are to be believed.'

'But so am I. The business has improved significantly. Why is my share still languishing at a third of its previous highs?'

'Reddy sahib, everyone who comes to me has the same problem. I give them the same advice—always respect the market. It knows more than any of us. There must be some reason. Tell me more.'

'I had taken a FCCB of US$ 50 million which is due for redemption in 2015.'

'Hmmmm...and you don't have the money to pay for it?'

There was deafening silence in the room.

'Don't get me wrong Reddy sahib, isn't that the reason you are here?'

Reddy silently nodded his head without looking up.

'What is the conversion price of the FCCB into equity?'

'Rs 450.'

'Your share currently trades at less than half of this value. Am I right?'

Reddy again nodded his head in concurrence.

'Don't look so sad, Reddy sahib. Cheer up! You have built a great company. You should be proud of your achievements. Let no one tell you otherwise.'

Reddy immediately looked up and asked, 'So, can it be done? Will you help?'

'Of course it can be done. I have done it in the past for paper companies which had no business, assets or employees. In contrast, your company has a solid business and assets deployed the world over.'

'What do we need to make it happen?'

'We need a story, planning and some money.'

'Is that it? I already have a great story.'

'Not your existing story. We need a new story. The market doesn't like your existing story. It suspects that you will default and is therefore not giving you your due valuation.'

Salil-bhai stood up. It was time for his next meeting. He shook Reddy's hand and said—

'Go back home and relax. We have time on our side, almost three years to get this right. Mull over it and call me when you have an idea. Anything that helps to improve your cash flows.'

'But why would anyone believe my story?'

'It is now our story, Reddy sahib. Remember, the market is never wrong. When your share price moves up, everyone will be forced to believe in our story.'

And Salil-bhai walked back to the adjoining room.

'Sorry about the delay, sir,' he said. 'But Modi sahib was just not willing to leave.'

Money Talks and Bullshit Walks

They assembled in the seminar hall a few days later to listen to the young and dynamic CEO of TBB Limited. His name was Sunny and he was only 29 years old.

'I remember sitting in a similar hall a few years earlier and listening to the placement talk of TBB Limited,' he said. 'If you had asked me then, whether I would become the CEO of this company at such an early age, I would have replied in the negative. But I didn't know then what I know today. We are meritocracy driven.'

There was loud applause in the room.

Sunny was young, but he had already walked the path of success in the adult world, unlike the boys and girls who sat before him and who still seemed to be in their adolescence. Sunny had seen the worst that would have turned them white and done much worse. He went on.

'We grew at over 50 per cent last year. If you are seeking growth, then this is the job for you. However, such exponential growth comes with its drawbacks. We are unstructured and there is pressure on performance. The learning curve is steep and most will fall behind.'

The smile on Devika's face widened. She had found her dream job.

'We entice our clients to buy and sell stocks. However, the final decision always rests with them. Why stocks, you may ask? Because, stocks have delivered better returns than any other class of assets. Hence, you are selling the right product. Make no mistake about it.'

Anil yawned, he had little interest in this bullshit. All he wanted to know was if they would offer him a job.

'We are competitive and performance is judged by numbers. We believe in giving cash rewards. No "thank-you" notes or flowers, just simple money. As they say, money talks and bullshit walks. If you are not motivated by money, don't join us.'

Sunny stopped speaking for a few seconds, allowing his audience to absorb what he had just said.

'If you don't like what you have heard so far, feel free to leave this hall.'

Pooja looked perplexed. She wasn't excited. On the contrary, she was quite disturbed. How could a person be motivated only by money? This was alien to her way of thinking. She was definitely a misfit.

She looked at Varun, expecting him to stand up and walk out. A dozen students left the seminar hall, but Varun was not amongst them. His eyes were fixed on Devika, who seemed to be mesmerised with the speech.

Sunny walked away from the mike and gestured to his associates to take over the recruitment process.

'It is simple and straightforward. All you need to do is to introduce yourself with specific emphasis on your social network. Tell us about your school, college, extracurricular activities and hobbies. Keep it short and sweet, no more than two minutes per person.'

It was all over within the next two hours. Fifty out of the fifty-eight students had been selected. Pooja, Varun, Devika and Anil had all made the cut.

'Is that it?' asked Pooja, a little bewildered. 'We have the job?'

'Of course, we have it,' yelled Anil in excitement. 'I am getting drunk tonight.'

'What a sham,' she said. 'A two-minute chat and we are in.'

'Don't you undermine my accomplishment!' retorted Anil.

'No one is compelling you to join,' said Devika.

Varun looked pensive. There would be shock and anger when he broke the news to his parents. He put his arm around Anil's shoulder, and said, 'Yeah, let's go out and get a few beers, buddy.'

'You girls want to join in?' asked Anil.

Pooja waited for Devika's response.

'Thanks! But I have other engagements,' she replied.

'I am feeling tired. I guess I should also be heading back home,' said Pooja.

There are No Winners, Only Survivors

Sunny left the placement session smiling broadly. He was rather pleased with the results.

'Sir, do you think that all of them will turn up to collect their offer letters?' asked one of the younger associates, who had only recently joined the organisation and was attending her first placement talk.

'Yeah, most of them will. I could see some of them moving excitedly in their chairs. The trick is to make it sound challenging but rewarding. This excites people with a particular trait, the killer instinct.'

'But do you think all of them qualify for this category.'

'Not all of them. Some will join us because they don't have any other option. Then there are the fence sitters, the confused lot who like the reward but aren't sure if they will survive the rigour. There will also be a few go getters.'

Sunny excused himself and went off for a smoke, allowing the two associates to continue their conversation.

'Maybe we should have conducted interviews to identify these go getters?'

'Interviews are useless,' replied the senior associate. 'Kids these days prepare for interviews. They all give well-rehearsed answers. How can you judge the character of a person in a 15-minute interaction?'

'But at least we could have asked them about their performance at school?'

'How does that help? There is no correlation between the two. For any non-technical job, all you need is logic and soft skills, neither of which are taught at a business school. I would much rather throw these kids in the deep end and wait patiently to see who survives.'

Sunny returned just then and caught the tail end of the conversation. He could see that the younger associate wasn't convinced.

'Listen, I know all this sounds unorthodox. All I know is that if a person has done his schooling and college in a city, then over a period of 15-20 years, he ends up meeting 300 to 500 new people. Let's call this his network. All fifty of them start with this network. Thereafter, how well they exploit this network to source business for our organisation is a function of their individual skill and motivation.

'In the first month, we will teach them the basics. You will see smiles on their faces, laughter and chatter will fill the office, even the occasional flirting.'

'Sir, you mean we will babysit them?'

'Yes, exactly. This will be their honeymoon period.'

'In the second month, there will be pressure on them to get new clients. Based on my past experience, each of them should get twenty new accounts. One in every ten will be a High Net-Worth (HNI) client. This is the client we want, the client who is profitable. I have tried and tested different recruitment processes in the past and arrived at the conclusion that there are no short cuts to this process.'

'Ok, fair enough. But they haven't yet generated a single rupee of revenue.'

'Hold on to your horses, lady. Revenue will happen in the third month. We will kick their ass red, abuse the shit out of them and hound them continuously to generate revenue. They will fall, left, right, and centre. Some will crack under pressure and you will see a few emotional breakdowns. They will look like zombies, some will stop sleeping, whereas others will lose their appetite. Make no mistake, they all fall down. There are no winners in the third month, but there will always be a few survivors. I don't expect more than 10 per cent of this lot to remain in the organisation at the end of the third month.'

'Only 10 per cent? That's inefficient, isn't it?'

'Ha-ha! Certainly sounds irrational, doesn't it. Paying salaries to fifty people for three months, knowing in advance that only 10 per cent will remain. But there is logic in this madness. These guys will collectively introduce 1000 new clients to the organisation. Approximately, a 100 of these will be HNIs. These clients will provide the fodder on which the organisation will feed.'

'What about the existing lot of relationship managers?'

'They are lazy. They seldom venture outside the office to meet new clients.'

'Why don't we fire them?'

'We can't fire them. They meet their revenue numbers. In fact, they are most efficient in generating revenue. Hence, we feed them with new clients to exploit.'

The Eerie Calm Before the Storm

'Son, have you packed your bags?' asked Mr Aggarwal.

'No, I haven't papa.'

'Aren't you cutting it fine? You are supposed to leave for Baroda tomorrow, aren't you?'

'No papa, I am not.'

'Why? What happened? Has the date of joining been pushed back?'

'No. I have refused their offer.'

'You aren't joining the textile company? Why? Have you found yourself another job?'

'Yes, I have. This one is based out of Delhi, and I start only next week.'

'That's great! Your mother will be thrilled. She was worried sick as to how her beloved son would cope in a new city. Which company are you joining?'

'It is called TBB Limited.'

'TBB Limited? Haven't heard of them. What do they do?'

Varun stopped fiddling with his bag and took a deep breath. He sat down on the bed and looked his father in the eye.

'The Big Bull Limited. It is a stock broking firm.'

There was stunned silence in the room. His father was speechless. Varun wondered whether he should repeat himself. Then the anger and raw emotions burst out. His mother came running from the kitchen and saw her husband shouting uncontrollably while her son listened to him calmly.

'You left a textile job to become a *dalal*?' cried his father. 'Are you mad? What were you thinking? This industry destroyed our lives. You had the whole world before you. Why did you take this job? You know what happened to us!'

He went on and on for the next few minutes. Finally, his throat became hoarse and he stopped. Varun calmly stood up and poured him a glass of water.

'Don't blame the industry for our misfortune,' he replied. 'Some people have also made significant wealth in the stock markets. Look at our neighbour, Mr Arora. You both started out together. But today he is in a different league altogether. He swears by the stock markets.'

'Oh! My son attaches more importance to a neighbour's advice. Young man, Arora is not paying your bills, I am. Your stupidity will haunt us tomorrow, not him.'

'Papa, I respect you. But you must allow me to walk my own path.'

'Not when I know that it is riddled with thorns.'

'Papa, you are biased in this matter. The retail broking industry offers great opportunity for growth. I have thought this through before making my decision.'

'Like you did the last one, ending in that business school. Good money gone bad.'

'I will return your money. I didn't want it in the first place. I wanted to take a loan, but you insisted.'

Mr Aggarwal lowered his voice and spoke in a conciliatory tone—

'It is not about the money, son. Listen to me and write back to that textile company. It's still not too late.'

'Papa, I made the mistake of joining the business school without proper diligence and have suffered the consequences. I made the best of the limited opportunities available to me on the campus and didn't come begging to you for a job. I have made up my mind. You need to learn to trust me more. There is no turning back now.'

'Then do as you please,' his father replied angrily. 'But don't you come to me asking for help. This decision is yours alone, not mine.'

Why do We Need the Police?

A month after they collected their offer letters, they found themselves cramped in a small shabbily furnished room which had only recently been converted into a makeshift class room. They were to spend one week of orientation here, attending lectures.

Devika was amused that despite her reservations, Pooja had decided to join.

'Hello Pooja, I am surprised to see you here. Didn't I tell you, I have become quite a trend setter,' she said sarcastically.

'Dream on! I didn't follow you here.'

'Of course you didn't,' she replied, looking pointedly at Varun.

They spent the first day learning about the account opening kit. The damn thing required 55 signatures, miss one of them and the entire kit was rejected. It was a bulky and cumbersome document. This was not without reason. Clients seldom read the entire document. Those who did, never signed it. It was one sided, the client acknowledging that he didn't have any rights whatsoever. The only thing he was left with by the time he signed the 55th time, was his soul, and that too only because the organisation hadn't yet figured out how to monetise it.

Varun made a note in his diary, "*Must count the signatures before leaving the client. Otherwise, you will be hauling your ass back to the client's house.*"

The next day, they interacted with the risk management department (RMS). Relationship managers feared them and kept them in good humour. RMS decided on the size of investment in the market. This investment amount could vary depending on the amount of borrowed funds. Customers could borrow funds based on the collateral value of their cash balance and shares held with the broker. The size of investment had a direct bearing on the amount of commission income that could be earned. Since borrowed funds were involved, RMS had to monitor client positions in real time, including chopping off those positions which were deemed dangerous of going under i.e. out of money. While there were rules to guide them, the final decision was subjective and open to bias. Consequently, they enjoyed autonomy with little accountability. Their actions were often erratic and were never challenged.

Varun made another small note in his diary. "*If they like you, your position will stand. Otherwise, may lord have mercy on your soul!*"

It was the turn of the compliance department to meet them on the third day. Compliance was responsible for defining the rules and regulations, and policing them to ensure adherence. It was a thankless job. Whoever liked the Police? Luckily for them, they weren't in a popularity contest. Otherwise, they would have lost even before the contest began.

If you believed the relationship managers, then compliance was a pain in the ass, always fingering them and making their job of selling to the clients difficult. It mattered little to the relationship managers that they were constantly breaking rules in their quest to generate higher revenue, especially so when no one was looking.

It was a cat and mouse game between them. Relationship managers tried their best to exploit every possible lacuna to improve their performance. The methodology didn't matter. Compliance was always a few steps behind them, but soon caught up with their act and closed the loophole.

Varun jotted down in his notebook, 'Why do we need policing?'

The last two days were spent with the sales department. The amount of commission income, known as brokerage income in share market parlance, that a broker could earn was directly related to the rate of commission and the size of investment. An intelligent relationship manager knew that half the battle was won at the time of account opening by charging the client a higher rate of brokerage. If you were lucky to run into a virgin client who had no clue about the markets, you could charge him a rate of brokerage as high as 2.5 per cent on *delivery trades* i.e. trades that were not nullified before end of day. This was the maximum brokerage permissible by the regulator. However, in today's decadent society, where bastards roamed the streets, it was almost impossible to find such virgin clients.

While the rate of brokerage was lower on intraday trades which had to be nullified before the end of the day, one could use borrowed funds or leverage to increase the size of the investment. Every broker provides at least six times financing on intraday trades, buying and selling securities the same day to increase the volume or turnover of trade to raise their commission. Hence, for every Rs 100, one can buy shares worth Rs 600.

Using borrowed funds or leverage was a two-sided sword. In the right hands, it could increase the amount of profit earned by a client by increasing the size of his investment. But in the hands of a novice its impact was devastating, often wiping out large chunks of the client's capital. 'Stop-loss' was a safety mechanism introduced to protect the capital of clients from adverse leverage trades. It was akin to a safety lock on a gun.

Varun jotted down in his diary—"*Must inculcate the habit of putting a stop-loss on every leverage trade.*"

At the end of the first week of orientation, the four of them met at a local bar to exchange notes.

'Which session did you enjoy the most?' asked Pooja.

'I found the bit about leverage exciting,' replied Anil. 'No pain, no gain.'

'I second that,' said Devika. 'Leverage used along with a "stop-loss" can be an effective tool to increase revenue.'

'I think all the sessions were informative,' said Varun. 'To trade, you need to first learn how to open an account, don't you?'

'Stop giving *gyaan*,' replied Anil.

'What about you Pooja? Which session did you like?'asked Devika.

'Compliance,' she replied.

Anil almost choked on his beer.

'Compliance? Are you serious?' he laughed loudly. 'I struggled to keep my eyes open. God knows how many chewing gums I had to stuff into my mouth.'

Devika also decided to take a dig. She never missed an opportunity to pull Pooja down.

'Ha-ha! Oh my darling, you are so predictable,' she laughed.

But Pooja wasn't going to give in.

'I am serious guys,' she replied. 'It might not be a bad option to consider.'

'Oh! So now you have decided to switch camps?' asked Devika. 'Last I remember, we were on the same side.'

'Not yet, I haven't,' she replied. 'But it's an option that I would like to explore.'

'What's up buddy? You've gone quiet. Pooja is considering switching camps, and you have nothing to add,' said Anil.

'It's because of you,' said Devika. 'Stop pulling his leg. We are missing your pearls of wisdom, Varun.'

Varun looked up at the three of them. 'Guys, none of you is asking the right question.'

'See him bounce back,' said Devika, smiling. 'Why don't you enlighten us?'

'Why do we need compliance? Why do we need a department to police us? Why do relationship managers commit fraud and deceive?'

There was silence on the table as they considered an appropriate answer. The more they thought about it, the more questions arose in their mind. Was this going to be a way of life for them? After a minute had elapsed, all of them were staring blankly at their glasses of beer, much like Varun had done earlier.

'Mr Serious, look what you have done! Your lecture was so serious that it has rubbed off on all of us,' laughed Devika, making light of the conversation.

Meanwhile, Anil ordered another round of drinks.

Drinks flowed freely that night. But it didn't matter how much they drank, the damage had been done. The question churned inside their gut, piercing most of them like a needle, reminding them that all was not well.

They didn't know it then, but alcohol was to become a regular companion, helping them gloss over their daily worries, dull their conscience and sleep.

The Circus Called the Trading Room

On Monday morning they assembled at the reception and each one was handed an envelope. It contained the name of a relationship manager whom they had to shadow for the remainder of the month.

Varun excitedly opened his envelope. He had been anxiously waiting for this moment. Enough of classroom mumbo jumbo; finally, some practical hands-on training. He saw the name Atul Tiwari scribbled on the piece of paper.

'Ma'am, who is Atul Tiwari,' he asked?

'Oh! You have been assigned to Tiwari-ji,' she smiled.

'Mr Atul Tiwari?'

'Yes! We fondly call him Tiwari-ji.'

Anil overheard the conversation and laughed loudly. 'It appears, Mr Serious, that you have been assigned to Baba-ji.'

'Shut up,' retorted Varun.

'Ma'am, any idea where I can find Baba...I mean Tiwari-ji?' he asked.

'He should be in the trading room. As a matter of fact, so should all the other relationship managers. The markets are about to open in a few minutes.'

'Thank you, ma'am,' replied Varun, rushing towards the trading room.

'Just a word of caution,' said the receptionist. 'I would watch my steps inside that room.'

'Sure, thanks!'

Varun smiled back.

Anil put a hand on his shoulders. 'Buddy, where are you heading? Didn't you just hear what she said?'

'I did. But I want to be in the midst of the action,' he replied. 'I have waited too long for this moment.'

'So have we,' said Pooja. 'But let things settle down a bit and then we all can go in together.'

'Why do you guys have to be pussy all the time?' replied Varun, a little irritated.

Pooja was shocked at his retort.

'Let's go, Varun,' said Devika, with a big smile. 'I am also excited.'

Anil and Pooja went off to the pantry to grab a cup of tea, while Varun and Devika headed for the trading room.

Varun paused at the door apprehensively, the voice of the receptionist still reverberating in his ears. Devika, on the other hand, cool as a cucumber, opened the top button of her blouse deliberately—first impressions were important.

Then Varun opened the door, Devika by his side, and a sudden hush fell in the room. He wondered if it was his imagination, but for a brief moment life appeared to have stood still as every male eye in the room admired his companion.

Then time ticked on again and the usual high decibel frenzy filled the room again. In the midst of the mayhem, somebody yelled, 'Fucker, who's going to shut the door behind you, your Paa?' Varun turned round to close the door, and Devika disappeared into the crowd. He found himself in the centre of the trading room, people running in all directions, barking at the top of their voices, some on their mobile phones, while others just appeared to bark senselessly.

He looked around for Devika, but couldn't see her. Unknown to him, she stood calmly in one corner of the room laughing at the circus in front of her, while Varun seemed to be playing the role of a clown perfectly.

He was pushed and jostled from one side to another. Again and again he found himself in the way of people in a great hurry, who cursed him for blocking their path. By the time he managed to walk to the corner of the room, cold sweat was running down his temple.

He felt unnerved by the experience. The last time he was pushed around and manhandled in this manner was when he had tried to board a local train at Churchgate in Mumbai during the peak hour. It was a disaster. He had successfully boarded the train only after missing a few earlier ones. He stood squeezed between human flesh, smelling armpits and feeling a great sense of achievement, but he was pushed out at the very next station along with hordes of people who were getting off. It didn't matter that this was not his station. He tried to resist the push of the crowd, but he was cursed and shoved harder. It was futile to resist the exodus.

But even that experience was nothing compared to what he had just witnessed. He had never seen such urgency, energy and excitement. He stood dumbfounded in a corner of the room that he had finally managed to get into, catching his breath and trying to figure out his next move. Somewhere, in the midst of all this pandemonium was his mentor, his supposed guardian. He looked around helplessly until he spotted a man with chai.

Gliding through the mayhem was a peon carrying a tray filled with cups of tea. He walked with confidence, without an iota of fear through the storm around him. He was in demand and was received with much love and affection. Everyone loved tea, the elixir that calmed the nerves of the trading room.

This was his chance. Varun leaped towards the peon, took a cup of tea and asked, 'Boss, can you tell me where to find Atul Tiwari?' The peon gave him a blank look. Varun immediately realised his mistake and rephrased his question.

'Boss, where can I find Tiwari-ji?' he asked.

The peon smiled. He pointed his hand in a general direction and moved on distributing tea to the others.

Armed with the vague coordinates, Varun proceeded in the said direction and occupied the only available chair by a table. He looked around. Next to him sat a very busy man who was multitasking. In one hand, he held a fixed line phone and in the other his mobile phone. He was barking into the mouthpiece of the fixed line phone, getting the investment amount approved for a client while simultaneously confirming the amount to the client on his mobile. He had such ferocity in his voice that Varun dreaded the thought of him being on the other side.

Could this person be Tiwari-ji, he wondered?

There was only one way to find out. But his instincts told him now was not the time to disturb this man or make conversation with him. He waited impatiently for a few minutes, hoping that the gentleman would acknowledge his presence. But then, his patience ran out.

'Tiwari-ji, my name is Varun,' he said.

Before he could say any more Tiwari-ji retorted, 'You think, I give a fuck? And who gave you permission to warm your ass on that chair?'

What an Idea, Sirji!

Reddy had been tossing and turning restlessly in bed for the past two hours. He was tired and on any other night would have fallen asleep. But tonight his mind was not at peace. He ran the idea again and again through his mind, trying to poke holes in it. The idea was good and stood its ground. Actually, it was quite brilliant.

It had come to him in the middle of the night, waking him from deep slumber. For the tenth time in the past hour, he looked at his watch and frowned: it was only five in the morning. In another hour, the sun would be up. He could then go for a stroll. Anything to kill time.

He was excited. Earlier he would have dialled Salil-bhai irrespective of the time of day. However, experience had made him patient.

When the clock struck nine, he could no longer hold himself back. He pulled out the visiting card from his wallet. It looked like any other card, except that it didn't have a name on it, only a number. He anxiously dialled the number. The phone rang a few times but there was no response. After a minute, he received a call from an unknown number.

'Is this Mr Patel?' asked the unknown male voice at the other end.

'No. Wrong number,' replied Reddy. However, before he could disconnect the call, the voice asked again, 'Is that you, Mr Reddy?'

'Yes. It is,' he replied.

'Just hold on, sir.'

'Reddy sahib, *bolo*,' said the familiar voice of Salil-bhai. 'I believe you have a story to tell me.'

Salil-bhai went straight to the point, wasting no time on pleasantries.

'Yes, I do,' said Reddy. 'I will sell my drilling rig'.

'Won't that impact your operation?' asked Salil-bhai.

'No, it won't,' replied Reddy. 'It will be a sale and lease back arrangement. The rig will continue to be in operation. Only the ownership will change.'

'What an idea, Sirji,' replied Salil-bhai. 'What will be the impact on cash flow?'

'It will be cash flow positive. It's an old rig and after paying back the bank loan, I think we should be left with 10-15 million US$ cash, or maybe more. But definitely not enough to pay back the bond holders in entirety. Also, it will take time to find a buyer,' said Reddy.

'It doesn't matter,' said Salil-bhai. 'When are you announcing the quarterly results?'

'Next month.'

'Make sure you announce your intention. But be vague. Say you are in preliminary discussions to sell and lease back the rig.'

'Will the investors buy the idea?' asked Reddy.

'They will lap it up. We need to sort out the formalities and get started immediately. We don't have time.'

Hang on to Your Wallet

Varun stood at attention observing Tiwari-ji go through his morning schedule, barking on his mobile phone, speaking with one client after another. He was busy narrating what seemed like a well-rehearsed speech on the expected market opening. As he finished speaking with the last client, he gestured to the dealer who was sitting next to him to get ready to receive client orders.

As soon as the clock hit 9.15 am, the markets opened and the dealer received the first phone call from the client. He knew exactly what had to be done. Time was precious and hence no pleasantries were exchanged. He listened carefully to the client order, repeated it on the recorded line for clarity, then keyed the order into the trading terminal and smashed the phone down, all within 30 seconds.

'Buy 1000 shares of Deliance Industries at market price in my Client ID 12345,' said the client.

'Sir, I am buying 1000 shares of Deliance Industries trading at Rs 975 in your Client ID 12345. Please confirm?'

'Yes. Proceed.'

He kept repeating this process for the next few minutes. By the time the clock had hit 9.20 am, five different trades had been keyed into the trading terminal. Five more minutes later, three of the five trades had already been nullified or squared off. Two trades had made money, one had resulted in a loss, the stop-loss being triggered.

By 9.25 am, Tiwari-ji was relaxing in his chair whistling a happy tune. He had already achieved a turnover of over 1 crore and made an approximate brokerage commission of Rs 5000.

He turned round to see Varun still standing at attention.

'This is how we do business,' he said. 'Why are you standing like a policeman? Sit down, *baba*.'

As Varun sat down, Tiwari-ji took a deep, long whiff and looked at him approvingly.

'Nice perfume. Expensive?' he asked.

Varun just smiled and began to introduce himself again, but was gestured to stop.

'I heard your name the first time,' he said. 'Are you a management trainee here?'

'Yes sir, I am.'

'Why did you join this organisation? Was it the only job you had?'

'No sir, I declined another offer to take this job,' replied Varun.

'Oh! You had a choice? What made you join us?'

'The markets have always fascinated me,' replied Varun. 'I hope to become a Portfolio Manager someday, and make money for my clients.'

'What? A Portfolio Manager!' laughed Tiwari-ji, 'That's a first! Do you smoke?'

'Yes, I do.'

'Good. Go downstairs, buy a cigarette and wait for me. I will join you in a minute.'

Varun did as he was told. He didn't have to think about the choice of brand, for he was already carrying a packet of a respectable brand of cigarettes with him.

As soon as he saw Tiwari-ji walking down the stairs, he quickly pulled out his packet of Classic Milds and offered it to him.

Tiwari-ji gave him another look of approval, pulled out a few cigarette sticks from the packet and put them in his top pocket. He then lit a cigarette and took a deep drag.

'Are you from a rich family?'

'No, I am not,' replied Varun, surprised.

'I thought, maybe you are. You wear a new shirt, put on an expensive perfume and carry a packet of cigarettes, whereas most of us just bum sticks. You stand out in this crowd.'

Tiwari-ji didn't know that Varun had saved every penny he could of his pocket money for the past year to look the way he did, sacrificing movie nights, parties and eating out.

'If you are not rich, then I guess this job matters to you?'

'Of course, it does. My life depends upon it,' replied Varun.

'Ok. In that case, I will cut through the chase and get straight to the point. Did you see anyone who looked like a Portfolio Manager in the trading room?'

'I don't know.'

'Be frank with me, Varun, before I start having doubts about your intelligence.'

'No. I don't think I did.'

'Those guys upstairs are hustlers, not Portfolio Managers. They are financial mercenaries who can do anything for money. I would watch out for my wallet, if I were you.'

These weren't the words of encouragement that Varun was seeking, and he looked confused and uncertain.

'I am sorry to have burst your bubble. If you wish to become a Portfolio Manager, this is the wrong job for you. We are not in the business of making money for clients. Do you understand?'

'Yes, I do,' he replied.

But he didn't.

'Great! So now, let me tell you what it is that we actually do: we induce clients to trade. Sometimes a trade does make money for the client. But this is only incidental. Our objective is to generate turnover or volume by giving trading ideas to clients and making them trade. The higher the turnover we generate, the more brokerage commission we earn. Whether a client makes money or not is irrelevant.'

Varun looked blankly at Tiwari-ji, his mind in a whirl. His ideas about stock trading had been turned upside down. Had he made the right career choice? Maybe his father had been right after all. Had he messed up again?

'Sorry for being so blunt, but it's better now than later. This is a whore house. People get screwed here day in and day out. Usually, it is the clients who get screwed, but if you are not careful, it might be you. Still following me?'

'I am,' replied Varun, now nodding his head firmly.

'I cannot teach you anything about making money for clients. However, I can guide you on how to make them trade and at the same time save your ass while doing so.

'One more thing, never repeat the words 'Portfolio Manager' in that trading room again. Otherwise, you will be a laughing stock.'

Varun nodded.

'Let's head back upstairs and see how the trades have performed. Two of them were still live when I came downstairs for a smoke.'

'Weren't you worried leaving the room while trades were still live?'

'Not really. It depends upon the clients. In this particular case, they are experienced and know what to do. In case the market moves, either the target will be achieved or the stop-loss will get triggered. In either case, the trade will be squared off and we will make brokerage income. That is the beauty about this business, we always make money, whether the client makes it or not.'

Back in the trading room, the dealer informed Tiwari-ji that all the trades had been squared off. He checked the level of the Nifty (the market index) and said aloud, 'My intuition was right today, the markets did move up.'

'I guess it's been a good day so far,' said Varun. 'All your clients have made money.'

'Yes, I agree. It's been a good day. We have managed to generate a good turnover within the first hour of market opening. And three out of five trades made money.'

Varun was perplexed.

'But you just said that your intuition was that the market would move up. Then why didn't all your clients make money?'

'Finally, an intelligent question! My intuition said that the market would move up. That's why three out of five clients had bought the index in line with the direction of the market. However, my intuition is not always right. So, I ensure that 40 per cent of the trades are always against my intuition, that way, even when I am wrong, some clients are always in the money.

'Observe me closely over the next few days. Catalogue my actions. Understand why I do a particular activity. Once you have familiarised yourself with all the office activities, we shall make a few client calls. Now go, and enjoy your honeymoon period. You won't get this chance once you join the rat race. See you tomorrow at 8.00 am.'

Varun left the trading room and called up Anil.

'Where are you, buddy?'

'Having a smoke downstairs.'

'Met your Baba-ji?' asked Anil as soon as Varun joined him.

'Drop it, man! His name is Tiwari-ji.'

'So have you figured out why they call him Tiwari-ji?'

'Yeah! Out of respect. All his peers are regional managers. But he actually declined to take on larger responsibilities. He loves trading.'

'Sounds like a pussy to me.'

'No, he is not. He is smart and knows his stuff. His heart lies in trading. He enjoys trading too much to give up the role of the individual contributor.'

'You believe that? That's a lot of cock and bull, dude.'

'On the contrary, he happens to be amongst the highest incentive earners in the organisation.'

'Oh really! Is he? Now he has my respect. You can't argue with numbers you know.'

'Enough about him. How was your day?'

'Cool. Met my mentor. The bastard was busy ogling Devika, only interested in finding out more about her. Asked me to introduce him to her tomorrow.'

'You did any work?'

'Yeah, little bit. Met the dealer, a sweet guy. But my mentor is a smart ass.'

'Maybe that was required,' smiled Varun.

'Yeah, I have a feeling about him. He is going to make my stay really memorable.'

'Where are the girls?'

'You know Pooja. She has been cramming the product policies since morning and has also been practising filling the account opening kit.'

'That doesn't surprise me at all,' smiled Varun. 'What about Devika?'

'Wouldn't you like to know?' said Anil smiling. 'She was busy flirting with her mentor, who seemed to be lapping up the attention. I am sure he will be dancing to her tune by tomorrow.'

'Yeah, I am sure about that too,' said Varun.

'Buddy, are you free for the day? Let's head out and watch a morning show.'

'You mean a porno? Which one are they playing?'

'Does it matter? As if you care for the plot line.'

'Ha-ha! I am feeling nostalgic. Haven't done it since I was in college.'

Sethji, Stop Siphoning Funds

Reddy arrived at the Taj Hotel to meet Salil-bhai. This time, his body language was positive, he looked relaxed and was smiling.

'Reddy sahib! Ah, good to see you again. You look good with a smiling face.'

'Thank you,' replied Reddy.

'Business is good?'

'Great.'

'Well, in that case show some profits.'

The smile disappeared from Reddy's face.

'Sethji, stop siphoning funds from the company. You need to start showing profits and paying taxes.'

Reddy nodded sheepishly.

'Over the next three years we need to grow at 15 per cent. Is this feasible?'

'Maybe,' replied Reddy.

'Great! We understand each other. At least on paper your business needs to grow by 15 per cent. Now tell me about the numbers.' said Salil-bhai.

'You mean the quarterly results?'

'No, *baba*. Those are for the analysts. The only numbers that are relevant for this exercise are details of your active shares in circulation. Tell me about your shareholding pattern? What does the promoter hold in the company?'

'Sixty-five per cent.'

'Sethji, that must be your official holding. How many shares are held in *benaami* accounts? We both know you have shares belonging to you but not held under your name. You know, shares held by your driver, peon, gardener etc.'

Reddy was quiet.

'Reddy sahib, a single glance at the shareholding statement is all I need to know the answer. Everyone knows that the shares held by *shell companies* are a front for the unofficial holding of the promoters,' said Salil-bhai. 'Everyone that is, except for the regulator. So, you might as well tell me.'

'Thirteen per cent,' Reddy said, sheepishly.

What about shares held by your friendly circles, i.e. friends and family?

'Maybe 4-5 per cent.'

'And how many shares are dormant?'

'What do you mean?' asked Reddy.

'Shares that are not in active circulation—shares in physical format, dormant shareholders etc. A good proxy for this would be to look at the unclaimed dividend register.'

'I am not really sure, Salil-bhai, but I guess it should be another 2-3 per cent.'

There was silence as Salil-bhai did a few calculations.

'You have 2 crore outstanding shares. If I add up all the above categories, it comes to 85 per cent. Thus your active shares in the market are 15 per cent i.e. 30 lac shares. At a price of Rs 200 a share, this translates into a value of Rs 60 crores. Am I correct, Reddy sahib?'

'Yes, broadly you are.'

'This is very doable,' smiled Salil-bhai.

'So, how do we proceed from here?' asked Reddy.

'Let's talk money first. You will transfer Rs 10 crores in cash to my contact person. Once this amount has been received, I will start buying shares of your company.'

'Rs 10 crores,' said Reddy, a little rattled.

'Sethji, you cannot eat in a five-star hotel and hope to pay the price of a dhaba. I will buy 10 per cent of the equity from you at Rs 150 per share. This transaction will be done on the exchange at the prevailing price in the market. Since the share currently trades at Rs 200, you will have to compensate me for the difference in the price, i.e. Rs 50, in cash.'

Salil-bhai studied Reddy's face.

'This will reduce my holding in the company,' said Reddy.

'Not your official holding. You will sell the shares from your *benaami* holdings. Then, you should use the money that I give you to increase your official holding in the company. I suggest you buy another 4.9 per cent from the market. The market loves creeping acquisitions by the promoter group. It reinforces the conviction of the promoters in the business.

'Are these terms agreeable, Reddy sahib?'

'Yes,' replied Reddy.

'Great. Please have the cash sent at the earliest.

'Also, from now on, I would like you to send me the "Bhav Copy" listing the shareholding of the company on a fortnightly basis. I don't want to see any shares being sold by you or your informed circles.

'If you have any spare cash after increasing your official holding, you should use it to shore up your holding in your *benaami* accounts. Once I become active in your stock, you will never see these prices again. All this needs to be completed before you announce the quarterly results.'

'I will certainly postpone the board meeting if that's necessary,' said Reddy.

'In future, for every share I sell in the market, I will let you sell one share. This will go on till all my shares have been exhausted. After that, you are at liberty to sell as you deem fit.'

Tiwari-ji—The Snake Charmer

Tiwari-ji followed the same routine every day. He started at 8.00 am with a refreshing cup of tea.

'Varun, tea activates my brain.'

Then he switched on the television and watched NNCB for half an hour, diligently noting down the events in the global markets. Every now and then, much to the amusement of the office, he got excited and abused one of the market participants.

Once he had the market levels, he called up two specific clients. These were not ordinary clients, but professional traders. He indulged in intellectual masturbation with them, trying to second guess their opinion on the expected market opening.

By now, his cup of tea was empty and he called out, 'Chhotu, get me another cup of tea.'

Varun once asked him how many cups of tea he consumed in a day.

'I don't know,' Tiwari-ji said. 'I don't keep count of things that come free.'

Armed with his cup of tea, he proceeded on his daily morning ritual of 'Chai pe Charcha.'

'What is the news from Mumbai?'

He walked around the trading room, making small talk with dealers and relationship managers to get the pulse of the market.

'Is the operator circle in Kolkata active?'

Everybody associated with the market had their own source of information. Over a period of time, by trial and error, relationship managers zeroed in on specific clients who had quality information—information that made money.

'What does your customer say about the market today?'

Every relationship manager wanted to find out what Tiwari-ji had heard from his two professional traders. Having gathered all the information, he settled down to prepare his sales pitch. If the view was overwhelmingly positive or negative, his intuition told him to take a contrary position.

Once the sales pitch had been prepared, he glanced through the Morning Report. This report listed the cash ledger balance and stock portfolio of all clients mapped to him. Based on the value of collateral i.e. cash and stock balance, exposure or trading limits were allotted to clients. Further, in case any of the ledgers had a debit balance, he highlighted these accounts to his dealer Raman, who would have the cheques collected.

'Why is there a debit in Aunty's account?'

'Which aunty?' asked Raman.

Everyone was an aunty or an uncle for Tiwari-ji.

'The one in Punjabi Bagh. You were supposed to have her cheque collected yesterday.'

'Oh! That aunty,' replied Raman. 'She will sell the shares today.'

'Make sure she does. Otherwise, risk department will square it off at 3.00 pm, and we will have another problem on our hands.

'Did you send the profit cheque to Raj uncle?'

'Yes, I did.'

'Varun, always send profit cheques to clients. It doesn't matter how small the amount. It reaffirms the client's belief in both the market and in your skills to generate income for him. Then, even if you lose money, he will always give you a second chance. Some smart ass relationship managers take advantage and send cheques to clients even if they have made no profit. Return 10 bucks to the client from his own money and he will give you a 100 more. It always works.'

Next, he called the risk department, massaging their egos.

'Don't forget me, boss. Please remember my clients.'

Intraday trades, by definition, had to be closed before the end of day. Generally, this meant 3.00 pm, i.e. 30 minutes before market closing. After that, the risk department was at liberty to cut your positions at any time it desired. If they favoured you, then your clients could carry the position till 3.15 pm. However, if they didn't, then as soon as the clock struck 3.00 pm, your positions were cut.

'Why are the last 30 minutes so important?' asked Varun.

'The markets are very volatile with wild swings in either direction during the first 15 minutes of market opening and the last 30 minutes before market closing. Every HNI client wants to trade during this volatility by utilising the maximum amount of borrowed funds. But these sons of bitches in risk start cutting the intraday positions at 3.00 pm, just when the market becomes volatile.'

'Why cut a trade if a client is making money?'

'Exactly my point. But try explaining it to the risk department. They just don't understand. The easier alternative is to buy a few cigarettes for the head of the risk department and send him a few jokes daily. By keeping him in good humour, I am able to manage a few extra minutes for my clients.'

When the clock hit 9.00 am, Tiwari-ji got busy on his mobile phone speaking with one HNI client after another, narrating to them the well-rehearsed morning pitch including his opinion about the market.

By 9.30 am, i.e. within 15 minutes of market opening, he had finished most of his work. He now relaxed, walked around the office with a cup of tea in his hand, gossiped with the receptionist, took the occasional cigarette break and so on. At 11.00 am he was back in his seat.

He now concentrated on the list of retail clients attached to him, slowly going through their stock holdings and ledgers, identifying stocks which had appreciated significantly in value. Retail clients were suckers for realising profits and were always willing to sell shares in which they had any notional profit. The money so realised could be utilised for making fresh purchases. In case an account had cash balance, Tiwari-ji called the client and gave him a new investment idea.

By 2.00 pm, Tiwari-ji joined the others for lunch. They did a pot luck every day. People seldom liked their own food and the pot luck provided them with variety. During this time, the positions in the market were handled exclusively by the dealers.

As soon as it was 2.30 pm, Tiwari-ji reoccupied his seat by the trading terminal and focussed closely on the market movement. By around 2.45 pm, he once again started calling his HNI clients, throwing them ideas, hoping to get one last trade out of them.

After the market closed, he ran through the rough ledgers in the trading terminal to see how his clients had fared during the day.

Some clients made money and others lost, but overall, if the net ledger reflected a positive balance, then Tiwari-ji was a happy man.

By 4.30 pm, he left the office, usually calling on a client before heading back home. Most relationship managers in the office followed a similar routine.

Multi-Bagger to Beggar

'Look at him,' yelled Tiwari-ji. 'Last fortnight his CEO was predicting a 10000 level on the Nifty Index. Now, that the markets have tanked, this guy is predicting a 6000 level. Tomorrow, if the markets move up again, he will go into hiding and the CEO will be back on television, reminding the viewers about his earlier prediction.'

Tiwari-ji was an experienced trader. He had learnt much at the cost of his clients' money. He knew that it wasn't easy to make money in the markets and to predict what they would do was next to impossible.

'Market movement in the short run is completely random. It's like playing roulette in a casino,' he said. 'But don't ever say this to your clients. They invest because they believe that the markets are rational even in the short run. The whole system functions on the premise that markets are not random, that there is an inherent logic that can explain every market movement.'

'But Tiwari-ji, I just heard an expert give reasons for the fall in the market yesterday,' said Varun.

'Oh yes! You don't need to be an expert for that.'

'What do you mean?'

'Anyone can explain the movement of the markets after the event has happened. It is done to reassure the public at large. It allows investors to sleep better at night and restores their faith in the markets.'

'Are you telling me that even I can do this?'

'Of course, you can. It is very easy. Every economy has six or seven key economic indicators, some positive and others negative. Every time the market falls, all you have to do is blame the negative indicators. Similarly, the day the market moves up, you can go out thumping your chest and talk about the positive indicators.'

'Are you saying that the expert was bullshitting?'

'The answer is complicated. Macroeconomic indicators and fundamental analysis are good tools to explain the movement of the markets over long periods of time when prices revert to the mean valuation. However, in the short run, prices can be depressed or exaggerated. It is not correct to use long term economic indicators to explain short term movements in the market.'

'Then, why on earth do they give explanations for these short term movements?'

'Because, retail investors have short investment horizons. They will bite the bullet only if they are convinced that the markets are rational in the short run.'

'But most retail investors have long investment horizons. I have heard them say so, on many occasions.'

'Ha-ha! They all get into the market to make a quick buck and take a punt. However, when the stock falls, they get trapped. They don't have the balls to take a loss, so they keep holding on to their positions and become long term investors by default.'

'Oh!' said Varun, bewildered. There was so much for him to learn.

'The only thing which can be said with certainty in the short run is that markets go up when there is liquidity, i.e. there are more buyers than sellers.'

'Thanks! That is a big secret revealed!' Varun said, sarcastically.

'That is the only truth. Everything else is a story created to explain the truth. Invest on the multi-bagger recommendations of these experts, and you will end up becoming a beggar.'

Like Them, Don't Love Them

'Retail clients are an important part of any client portfolio,' said Tiwari-ji.

'But they hardly generate any brokerage revenue,' argued Varun.

'Individually, maybe not. But their importance lies in their vast numbers. They provide stability when there is a downturn in the market.'

'How is that?' asked Varun.

'During a downturn, HNI clients significantly reduce their trading activities. It is the retail client who continues to buy small quantities. Also, they are low maintenance. They don't bother you in the morning, or towards market closing. You can deal with them at your own convenience. But you have to be careful, because they are novices. They trust you and are completely dependent on you. Therefore, you must handle them with kid gloves,' said Tiwari-ji. 'Don't ever offer them leverage products.'

'Surely we can offer the retail clients leverage with safeguards?' said Varun.

'What safeguards are you referring to?'

'Stop-loss.'

'Ha-ha! Is that what they taught you?'

'Yes. Why do you laugh?'

'Stop-loss is not meant for retail clients. Retail clients shouldn't be delving in leverage products at all.'

'But why, Tiwari-ji?'

'A retail client considers you the market expert. He trades on the comfort that you provide him. When you say buy, he buys and vice versa. He believes he is in safe hands and there is literally no risk in the trade. So, where is the question of putting a stop-loss? If you even so much as mention a stop-loss to a retail client, the entire hypothesis that you know what you are talking about falls on its head and the retail client will never trade.'

'Oh! This never occurred to me.'

'And one more thing—stop-losses work only when there is liquidity in the market. If markets are illiquid, like on days of panic, then sometimes they don't get triggered.'

'Good to know,' replied Varun. 'I thought it was fool proof. How about HNIs? We can offer them leverage products, right?'

'Of course. They will lap it up. The more leverage the better. However, you must be very careful while dealing with them, for they are both cunning and demanding. They will keep you on your toes.'

'Is there something I need to keep in mind?'

'Offer them trading ideas, but never vouch for a trade.'

'Tiwari-ji, what do you mean?'

'First of all, never enforce your opinion on them. Never say buy this or sell this. Instead, say this looks like a good buy. If they still have a contrary view, then so be it. Don't forget, as long as they trade, you will make money. One more thing, they are high maintenance.'

'High maintenance?'

'They will seek your attention when you are most pressed for time—at market opening and market closing, when volatility is highest.'

'Why deal with them at all?' asked Varun. 'All you have told me so far is that they are a pain in the ass.'

'That's true! They are a pain in the ass. But they are also the backbone of your career. A single HNI client can give you more brokerage revenue than 50 retail clients together. Hence, you have no choice but to sleep with them.

'What about professional traders?'

'What about them? They don't need you. They only need your infrastructure, fast trading terminals, highest possible leverage and the lowest possible rate of brokerage.'

'Should I target them?'

'Be my guest. They are low maintenance and also high revenue generators. Like them, but don't fall in love with them.'

'You make them sound like a beautiful woman,' said Varun. 'Like them but don't fall in love with them.'

'There is a reason for what I said. If you fall in love with them, they will become demanding. They will keep asking you for more, for higher leverage and lower brokerage. Then a day will come when they are no longer profitable.'

When the training ended, Varun was brimming with confidence. Tiwari-ji was a great mentor with an exceptional understanding of the markets and even better understanding of people. He made everything look so easy, never in a panic, always calm and re-assuring. It was obvious that Tiwari-ji loved to trade and that trading was in his blood.

The mentors assigned to Anil and Pooja were quite different. They were often themselves lost and struggling to find their bearing in the system.

Anil's mentor was always on edge, eyes red due to lack of sleep, liable to shout at the slightest provocation.

Pooja had been assigned to a woman who was perpetually drunk. It was her way of dealing with the pressure of the work.

I Know Hunger When I See it

It was a well-furnished office located inside a technology park on the outskirts of Ahmedabad. From the outside, it resembled a call centre. It had 24/7 power backup and heavy security at the entrance, including smart cards and CCTV cameras. Any media device, including smart phones, had to be left at the entrance before entering the premises. Each and every employee came through a reference and had worked at a similar setup before.

The main entrance and the two strong doors led to a very large hall in which there were over 200 terminals representing approximately 50 different brokerage houses in the country. The noise from orders being punched simultaneously into the keyboards was deafening. On any given day, they had a turnover of over Rs 2000 crores at this office alone. It was the heart of Salil-bhai's stock market operation and if insiders were to be believed, there were several others across the country, but none this large.

Salil-bhai sat in his glass walled office overlooking the hall below. He was examining the morning report that listed his positions across clients and the amount of pay-in (money to be received from sale) and pay-out (money to be paid for purchases). The markets were supportive and things were progressing well.

There was a knock on the door as Kunal, his trusted lieutenant, entered the room. 'We have received Rs 10 crores from that Reddy fellow,' he said.

'That was quick,' replied Salil-bhai, a bit surprised. 'I only met him last week.'

'Bhai, you must have made quite an impression on the poor bastard.'

'Maybe I did, but more likely, it reflects his desperation.'

'Should we commence buying?'

'Yes, but only Rs 10 crores at a time. Buy the next tranche only after you have received the fifty rupee difference in cash on the first tranche.'

'As you suggest, Bhai. Who do you think I should hand out this work to?'

'Split it between four to five brokers, but give the largest chunk to that new kid on the block.'

'Who? Do you mean Sunny?'

'That's him. He made quite an impression on me.'

'Why do you trust him with this big job?'

'I know hunger when I see it. He reminds me of my youth.'

'Why not go with the tried and tested?'

'We need to keep expanding our operations. But do tell him that he needs to prove worthy of my trust. Also say that you don't like him much.'

Trouble for Everyone Sooner or Later

Two weeks after the training, they were assigned to different teams, each headed by a sales manager who was responsible for keeping a tab on their performance. They were supposed to open 20 new client accounts in the first month. This task had kept them on their toes and thus they were meeting for the first time since the end of their training.

'How are you faring, buddy?' asked Varun, taking a large swig of his beer.

'Ok, I suppose,' replied Anil. 'I have over 25 trading accounts in the pipeline.'

'Wow! That's a great start.'

'Don't get excited, dude. They are still some way off from being opened. I am currently struggling with the bank accounts. Once those have been sorted out, I will focus on the other formalities.'

'Whose accounts are you opening?' laughed Devika. 'They don't even have bank accounts!'

'Milkmen, drivers, and other people who run small businesses like shopkeepers, lorry owners and so on.'

Pooja was baffled. 'Are you serious?'

'Bloody hell, I am. They are good clients. They have cash. Not much, but it will do. Most importantly, they are all dreamers and thus, compulsive gamblers.'

The three of them smiled at each other.

'Thanks guys for your support,' said Anil sarcastically. 'I will break your teeth if you smile like that again.'

'By the way, Pooja madam, what are you carrying in this school bag of yours?'

'A sales kit.'

'A what?' asked Varun.

'An account opening form, newspaper articles on stock market performance, a research report and a note on asset allocation. I have been making presentations on financial planning, you know.'

'Ha-ha! Madam, the time for teaching is over, please start opening accounts before they kick your ass,' said Anil.

'Oh! I am sorry. Didn't I tell you that I have already opened 12 accounts?' retorted Pooja.

'You were saying something, Anil?' laughed Varun.

'Madam, please forgive and forget,' said Anil sheepishly. 'Can I make a copy of that sales kit?'

Varun laughed loudly. 'You are now going to conduct a seminar for *milkwallahs*?'

Anil looked at Varun angrily.

'Devika, why are you checking your watch, again and again? Is it new?' asked Pooja.

Devika replied yawning, 'Guys, I must go. I have a date.'

'A date? Are you serious?' said Varun. 'We don't have time to eat and you are going on a date!'

'That's the least I can do for the poor fellow who has opened 10 accounts for me,' she replied. 'He is genuinely concerned that I might not make it beyond probation.'

'Who is this guardian angel?' asked Anil.

'My ex-mentor. I allow him to put his arms round my shoulders every now and then. It keeps him excited.'

'But that's sexual harassment,' exclaimed Anil. 'You are harassing the poor fellow.'

Devika grinned, shrugged and left in a hurry.

'Varun, how are you doing?' asked Pooja.

'The account opening guys are giving me hell. They keep rejecting my accounts over tiny issues. Yesterday, I had one of my accounts rejected for a small overwriting.'

'That's not a big problem, buddy,' said Anil. 'Just go to Jaykumarji, you know, the peon who serves tea. Give him a cigarette and he will do the needful. He can successfully forge any client's signature.'

'Oh! Wow! I need to speed up. I have only opened seven accounts, and those too for family and friends.'

'Are you crazy? Opening accounts for your dear ones,' said an agitated Anil.

Varun and Pooja looked confused.

'Oh! No wonder you guys were smiling when I mentioned my *milkwallahs*! You fools, even I could have opened accounts for my family and friends. But these accounts will get screwed next month when we are forced to generate revenue.'

'No. They will not,' replied Pooja.

'Ha-ha! Lady, what have you been smoking lately? Open your eyes and look around you. Every account gets fucked sooner or later.'

'I don't agree with you,' said Varun.

'Of course you don't. You have put your head inside the shit pot and are arguing with me that it is clean.'

'I am sure there is an intelligent way of managing clients,' said Varun forcefully.

'This is a lost cause. I am not going to waste my time arguing. But please do open accounts for some people outside your immediate circle.'

Varun wouldn't admit it, but he knew that he was on a slippery slope.

'Let's call for the bill, guys,' he said, ending the discussion. 'I have an early morning meeting with an Aunty-ji.'

'Aunty-ji?' asked Anil. 'Uncle's reference?'

'I guess you mean my father?' replied Varun. 'No dude, we haven't been on talking terms for some time. He threw such a stink the day I told him I was joining this place.'

'Oh! I didn't know,' said Anil. 'I am sorry.'

'We have a love and hate relationship. These days it's convenient to hate me. But he will come round in due course. He always does.'

'This old woman is a reference from one of my uncles. She is a widow. Her late husband used to invest in stocks.'

Varun didn't sleep well that night. He kept thinking about his talk with Anil. He had to meet new people and expand his network quickly.

He reached Aunty-ji's house at 8.30 the next morning. She was waiting for him, pacing anxiously in her living room. On the dining table was a stack of share certificates.

'Varun *beta*, I have no money. But I have a lot of these,' she said, handing him a bunch of share certificates. 'See if they make sense to you.'

Varun took a glance at them. They were all in the name of her late husband, who had died in 1994. This meant a lot of work. He had done his homework before coming for the meeting. He knew that a copy of the death certificate would have to be filed along with the share certificates in original, an affidavit, KYC (Know Your Customer) documents etc., establishing her as the sole inheritor of these shares.

But before that, he wanted to see if the shares were worth his time. He was afraid that most of the companies might have gone under in the past 20 years.

'Aunty-ji, I will examine them and get back to you in a week,' he said.

He stashed the certificates in the side pocket of his bag and left in a hurry. His next meeting was in 30 minutes. It was with an uncle, who like his father, worked in a bank, but unlike his father, was an ardent investor in the stock market. He hoped that this meeting would be more fruitful.

However, it was not to be. His uncle was very happy with his existing broker, whom he had known for many years. Finally, Varun had stumbled across someone who was happy with his broker. There was still hope for his family and friends. Thus, despite his uncle's refusal, he felt happy.

'Uncle, can you please give me a few references. You are a banker and must be meeting a lot of people?'

'Sure!'

He perused through his visiting card folder, pulled out a card and handed it to Varun.

'This card is worth its weight in gold,' he said. 'Call him up and give my reference.'

The card belonged to the DGM, Finance, of a Public Sector Undertaking (PSU).

'They are coming out with an Initial Public Offer (IPO). Many employees have stock options and are in need of a broker.'

'Thank you, Uncle,' said Varun, delighted. Perhaps he had found his big ticket to success.

He spent the next fortnight diligently following up with the employees of the PSU and opening as many accounts as he possibly could. He didn't know whether these accounts made commercial sense. But he didn't care. He had been given a target and he was going to meet it.

What a Bunch of Monkeys!

All month there was hectic activity on the trading counter of Reddy Oil & Gas. The average trading volume jumped tenfold with several bulk deals reported on the exchange. Reddy transferred 10 per cent of his *benaami* holdings in favour of Salil-bhai through several dozen transactions. He simultaneously increased his official holding in the company by 4.9 per cent, the maximum limit permissible in a year without triggering an open offer.

Thereafter, he proceeded to shore up his *benaami* holdings. However, he found it increasingly difficult to buy any more shares from the market without impacting the price. The easy availability of shares seemed to have disappeared from the counter and any further purchases would have affected the price. And Salil-bhai's instructions were crystal clear: 'Under no circumstances should the price move before the information was made public.'

Consequently, Reddy was not able to increase his *benaami* holdings as much as he would have liked. They now stood at a mere 7 per cent, much lower than the 13 per cent at the beginning of the month. The time had come to call a board meeting and announce the quarterly results.

All this activity in Reddy Oil & Gas had not gone unnoticed. The stock market pundits knew that something was cooking. But they weren't sure what it was and waited for more information to emanate from the company. As soon as the quarterly results were announced, they analysed the numbers, only to realise that not much had changed on paper. The numbers were similar to those reported in the previous quarter. They were disappointed. Perhaps the information lay hidden between the lines! They waited anxiously for the conference.

When Reddy arrived for the conference call, he was informed by the administrator that 40 analysts–more than half of the broking industry–were present. While some of them were present in person, others had dialled in. He was pleasantly surprised at the turnout. It had never happened before, not even during the hay days of 2007. Obviously, the activities of the past month had not gone unnoticed.

He basked in the glory and told them all they wanted to know. At times, even more than they had bargained for.

'How do you see the business environment?' they asked.

'It is looking good,' he replied. 'The competitive landscape has improved significantly.'

'Do you expect to grow?'

Reddy remembered his crisp discussions with Salil-bhai—'Show me growth.'

'Of course,' he replied confidently. 'A top-line growth of 15 per cent looks very much doable.'

'What's your outlook on the margin front?'

'Stop siphoning funds from the company, Seth-ji,' rang in his ears as he answered.

'We have implemented various saving measures. Their effect on the margin will be visible in the coming quarters.'

He looked at them smiling and nodding their heads diligently. What a bunch of monkeys. Then came the icing on the cake.

'We are also in early discussions to sell one of our rigs and lease it back.'

There was pandemonium in the room as the analysts all tried to get more details at the same time. But this time Reddy smiled and said no more.

The Great Potential

A day before the monthly closing records showed that Varun opened 42 accounts, more than double the target given to him. He had more than met his numbers, even though 35 of these accounts didn't have money. The IPO of the PSU was scheduled in six weeks i.e. after his probation ended. He didn't know whether he would still be around to enjoy the fruits of his labour. Of the remaining seven accounts, six had margin money of Rs 1,00,000 each, whereas the seventh would soon be funded with shares, of whose value he hadn't a clue.

He hadn't had time to look at the share certificates in his bag in the last fortnight. Now he took out the bunch and started typing their names on the website of the market exchange. He didn't find any match for the first six certificates. He wasn't surprised; he had expected this. Either the companies had gone under, which was the most probable cause, or they had merged into another company thereby changing their name.

On the seventh certificate he got a match. He excitedly opened the page to look at its price and was disappointed to note that it was a penny stock. He looked at the share certificate in his hand. He had 100 shares worth only Rs 130. He smiled ruefully. The value of these shares didn't even cover the cost of sending a courier to the registrar. He threw the certificate back into the bunch and continued his search. Finally, at the end of the pile, he found something that made the entire exercise worthwhile—100 shares of Intotys Technologies. He quickly checked its price. Wow! Bingo. He had finally hit gold. It traded at Rs 1200 a share. A 100 shares meant Rs 1,20,000. Now he had seven accounts to flaunt at his review meeting tomorrow and another 35 which had potential. Not just potential, great potential, he thought.

His sales manager, when presented with his list of clients, was not convinced of their 'great potential'. On the contrary, he felt that Varun was being cheeky and making fun of him.

'You are a smart ass, aren't you?' he said. 'You want me to believe that all these accounts with zero balance have great potential? I am going to pay special attention to your progress now, for sure.'

Varun knew what that meant. He was in for special treatment, unless he could somehow generate one month's pay as brokerage income. For the first time, he didn't crib about his meagre monthly salary of Rs 20,000.

Given that there were approximately 20 working days in the month, a revenue of Rs 1000 per day would suffice. Since, all his clients were on a delivery brokerage rate of 0.5 per cent, all he needed was a *delivery trade* of Rs 2,00,000 daily to meet his revenue target. This didn't sound that difficult, except for the fact that he only had six clients with money. The rest of them, including Aunty-ji had only high potential and nothing more.

This strategy of buying shares would work only for three days. What should he do thereafter, he wondered. He could always diversify, i.e. buy at least three different shares in his client's accounts and hope that at least one of them would perform. He could sell this share on the fourth day, and with the money generated buy another one on the fifth. This could go on week after week, so long as at least some of the shares kept growing in value. It wasn't the perfect plan, but it was a plan nevertheless. All he needed now was a little bit of luck.

He wasn't too worried as far as generating profits was concerned. All that was needed to be done was buy cheap and sell expensive. So long as the sale price was higher than the buying price, there was profit. Such a simple equation. He wondered why people hadn't thought of it. He slept well that night believing that all was under control.

The next day, he even smiled and wished his boss. He was being cheeky now and overconfident, but then, he had it all figured out, or so he thought.

What he did not know was that his boss had been regularly checking his trading terminal to figure out what he was up to, hoping to see him fail. It didn't take him long to figure out his plan.

On the fourth day, he gave Varun a bright smile. Varun reciprocated, because he knew that at least today he was safe. One of the shares in the portfolios had moved up, giving him the opportunity to sell. Varun's boss was disappointed to find that his greenhorn had survived another day. Lucky bastard, let's see how long this lasts, he thought.

The next day, Varun bought another share from the money generated by the sale of the previous day. The first week thus came to an end exactly as per plan. He wished his boss a good weekend, called it a day and proceeded to their favourite joint for a drink.

Where is the Fun in That?

When Varun reached the bar, he was surprised to see the two ladies quietly sipping their drinks.

'Amazing. No arguments today,' he thought.

'Where is Anil? He hasn't come yet?' he asked them.

'Nope,' replied Pooja.

'That's odd, he left at the same time as I did.'

A few minutes later, Anil walked in.

'Where were you, buddy? I think we left at the same time,' he asked.

'I had to take a few detours,' he replied.

'Why? Did you have some work?' asked Devika.

'No dude, I was avoiding the *cigarettewallahs*.'

'Don't tell me you have borrowed money from them?' said Devika.

'Only a little,' replied Anil.

Varun shook his head in disgust.

'We have only been here for two months and you have already started this nonsense,' he said.

'If it's only a little, then why don't you pay them back?' said Pooja.

'Where is the fun in that!' Anil replied.

Then quickly changing topic he said, 'Guys, did you know that Sunny and Jayant were friends once?'

'You mean Jayant, The Head of Operations?' asked Pooja.

'Yup! They used to be great friends earlier.'

'Wow! They don't see eye to eye at all now,' said Devika.

'Sunny was happy when Jayant joined operations. Who better than someone who understood the problems confronting sales? He thought life would become easier for him.'

'What happened? Why did they fall apart?' asked Varun.

'It depends on who you ask. Jayant felt that Sunny was taking advantage of their friendship. Sunny felt that Jayant was trying to create unnecessary obstacles in his growth. The rest is history. They fight like cat and dog now.

'Pooja, I hope we continue to remain good friends forever,' said Devika, sarcastically.

'Depends on you, darling,' Pooja replied, without mincing her words. 'I know how to reciprocate.'

'Stop it, you two!' said Anil. 'How is everyone faring? Who is leading the revenue charts?'

'She is,' said Varun, pointing towards Devika. 'But don't ask her how she reached that number.'

'Seriously! You guys have nothing better to discuss?' retorted Devika.

'What do you mean?' asked Anil, ignoring her.

'Her ex-mentor has been regularly trading on her behalf,' replied Pooja.

'You mean on the accounts that he had opened for her in the first place?' said Anil.

'Yeah,' she replied, laughing.

'Devika darling, what's been keeping you busy?' asked Anil innocently.

'A girl always has plenty to do,' she replied, holding out and examining her manicured hands. 'Don't look at that tomboy.'

Pooja scowled.

'How are you going to meet your numbers next month?' asked Varun.

'Why? Is there a problem? It's not as if I am not doing any work. I am learning how to trade from him. In any case, the last time I checked, there were enough idiots in the office. I am sure I will find someone else, if required.'

Smiling at Anil, she asked, 'How are your *milkwallah*s doing buddy?'

'Great! They are on auto pilot mode. I don't have to do anything. They are like rabbits, they keep fucking the whole day, calling me up only for new trading ideas. Their trading limits are always exhausted and on three different occasions last week the risk guys had to chop off their positions.'

'Wow! That sounds interesting. Are they making any money?' asked Varun.

'I don't know. But they are certainly enjoying trading. And you? How are you faring? Burnt any of your aunts and uncles yet?' asked Anil.

'Touch wood' replied Varun. 'I have been lucky so far.'

'Pooja Madam, what about you? How have you been?' asked Anil.

Pooja's eyes lit up as she began talking of the research reports she had read, the stocks she had identified. After listening to her for a minute, to the relief of everyone else, Anil interrupted, 'Ok, so I guess you are doing well.'

'Yes,' she replied.

'Please do share that list of stocks with us,' said Varun.

They sat there for another hour drinking and gossiping, unaware of the churning in the global markets.

Being Mature, My Ass!

There was anxiety on every face on Monday morning. The markets opened low with a 300-points gap over the previous closing. The prices of the stocks Varun had purchased plummeted before his eyes. He wondered what to do. His first instinct was to run to Tiwari-ji. But he stopped himself. He had broken every rule Tiwari-ji had taught him. He was at fault and would have to sort this out on his own.

Hoping for some guidance, he walked into the pantry and turned on the television to listen to the market experts. But they were of little help, one after another dolefully predicting the end of the world. After 15 minutes, he couldn't take their blabber anymore and shut the television.

He had no option left but to seek guidance from his boss.

'What happened, shit face? You are not smiling today,' said his boss sarcastically.

He ignored the sarcasm. This was not the time for one-upmanship. 'What should I do?'

No reply from his boss. Undeterred, he asked again, 'What are you doing?'

'Nothing,' came the reply. 'I am drinking tea. You would be doing the same had you not decided to become 'God' and play the Portfolio Manager for your clients. Now do as you deem fit.'

'But what are your clients doing?'

'Oh! My clients are selling in panic.'

Varun was in big trouble. He spent the next half hour running around the office, talking to people and trying to figure out what most people advised. He did not know that following a course of action based on majority advice was often very expensive. By the time everyone agreed that one should sell, the market was already at the low point of the day. Nevertheless, he went ahead and advised his clients to chop off all their positions.

For the next 30 minutes he felt relieved that he had made the right choice. Then, the market started to climb again. He rushed back to listen to the experts on the television and was comforted by their negative comments—this was only a temporary phenomenon and the market would surely fall tomorrow. However, by the time the markets closed that day, all the stocks that he had sold had climbed significantly.

He didn't sleep well that night, turning and twisting, praying that the markets would fall the next day. As soon as he woke up at 6.00 am, much earlier than usual, he switched on the television. The news was disastrous. The international markets had reversed the losses overnight and ended the day on a high. He frantically switched channels hoping that some of the experts who had predicted a fall yesterday would say something reassuring. To his dismay, the entire panel of experts had changed. The ones on television now were predicting that the market would open up with a gap over the closing level of the previous day.

'What the fuck? Bring back the bastards who were predicting doomsday yesterday,' he yelled.

'Watch your language, young man,' shouted his father from the bedroom. 'I can still hear you and this is my house.'

He dressed quickly and left for office. He did not want to face his father.

As soon as he reached office, his boss congratulated him.

'Good job, shit face! You generated a revenue of Rs 3000 yesterday.'

'But what should I do today? I sold everything yesterday in panic.'

'Simple. Buy it again,' replied his boss.

'Buy it again? How? What should I tell them? I will look like an idiot.'

'You are an idiot, shit face. You made a mistake yesterday and panicked, now you need to make it right.'

The market opened higher with a gap over the previous close. However, after a few minutes it fell down a bit. For some moments, Varun felt that all his prayers had been answered. But it was not to be as the market stabilised and once again resumed its upward journey.

Varun acted immediately and made up a cock and bull story to convince his clients to repurchase stocks that they had sold previously. They did as they were advised, but it was at a loss since the price of stocks had climbed significantly. So much for buying low and selling high.

His boss, who was keeping an eye on his actions, was amused. Revenue of Rs 3000 again, he wrote in his diary.

As the day ended, Varun told himself never to panic again. Two days later, when the markets tumbled again, he didn't panic and held on to his stocks. He was going to be mature about it. Unfortunately for him, the markets had other plans and continued falling day after day.

When his loss surpassed 10 per cent, he cut his entire holding of stocks. So much for being mature and not panicking.

Varun was now dancing to the tune of the market. It was Hip-Hop on some days, Reggae on others. Sometimes he bought, only to sell the next day. Sometimes he sold only to buy again. However, most often the purchase price was higher than the sale price. He felt as if the market was watching his every action and went up every time he sold, fell when he bought. His actions, which were made in good faith and judgement, looked completely ad-hoc and illogical. However, they did help him generate a lot of brokerage revenue.

He had acted against everything that Tiwari-ji had taught him. By the end of the month, he wished that he had listened to Anil and not opened the accounts of his family and friends.

Anil had fared much better. Not because his clients made money, but because they gambled without seeking his advice. Thus, he was not responsible for what happened to their money. Consequently, he slept well at nights.

However, Pooja was not so lucky. She, like Varun, had lost a lot of money for her clients. By the end of the month, it was amply clear to her that this wasn't her cup of tea.

Devika was oblivious to the happenings in the market, spending time shopping and in salons, getting her hair coloured. Her ex-mentor was not so fortunate, bearing the brunt of the fall in the market. However, she kept him happy by going out with him regularly for drinks and dinner. He paid the bill of course.

The Bliss of Ignorance

Varun sat alone looking blankly at the trading terminal in front of him. The office was quiet because the market had closed for the day and most of his colleagues had stepped out for a break. The relationship managers were smoking and discussing the happenings in the market, while the dealers ate their lunch in peace, away from the hustle bustle of the trading room.

Normally, he would have joined them for a smoke. But not today. Today was a special day; his period of probation had just ended. He had completed–or rather, survived–three long months in the organisation. Of the 50 students who had started this journey, only seven remained. The rest had either resigned or been fired. They had crumbled under the intense pressure, been humiliated and abused within the office for non-performance and hounded by clients, who had lost their hard-earned money at the hands of inexperienced nincompoops who couldn't tell their ass from their head.

It had been difficult. They had run around with barely any guidance or direction, trying to achieve almost impossible numbers. Devika was the only exception. She had found her own way of dealing with the organisation and navigating its maze.

Varun wasn't thrilled with his achievements. Neither was Anil, nor Pooja. However, only Pooja expressed her displeasure. The others shared her sentiments, but were scared of saying so. The company despised those who exhibited any form of weakness or dissent. Such people were humiliated and sacked.

He had survived, but at a big personal cost. His immediate circle of friends and relatives had been annihilated. Most of them no longer wished to speak with him and the few who did, didn't trust him anymore. How could they? He had lost their hard-earned money, gambled it away on trades that he knew very little about and understood even less. Money that he had promised he would help multiply, a promise that held little weight now. He could hardly face them now. On several occasions he took the back door just to avoid running into them. He was now glad that he had fought with his father, that his father had refused to help him. Otherwise, he too would have lost what little money he had.

"But I had the right intentions, I was well meaning and wanted to make them money..." he thought to himself. *"I would have succeeded,*

had I not been limited by my lack of knowledge or my rudimentary trading skills. It would have been all well today.

"I entered into a few more trades only to make good their loss.... Maybe, Papa was right....

"No. I can't give up. I need to do this differently. I can't let the pressure get to me. I must prove him wrong!"

So he approached a few of his seniors, the presumably learned lot, and asked them for tips about where to invest and how. He should have also asked them if they had ever made money for any of their clients, because the losses kept mounting with almost every trade. The more he applied himself, the more he lost. When almost half of all the client money given to him was gone, it finally dawned on him that the loss had become too large to recover.

He decided to approach this problem logically, going back to his friends and family and explaining to them the predicament that he was in.

'Give me some more money,' he said. 'Enough, that I can make good your loss.'

It was a mistake. As one of his clients told him later, much later when the damage had already been done, 'Boy, the last time you were here, you wanted to make us a profit and grow our capital. Now you only talk about recovering our loss. Don't you have confidence in your ability?'

How could he tell him that he had been confident when he was ignorant? He was wiser, therefore humble now.

He didn't get additional money from any of them. They were all good to him, still following the niceties, giving excuses when they could have been downright blunt and angry. If he had returned their money and accepted his mistake and apologised, they might have forgiven him, after a few late-night whiskies.

But instead, he did the unthinkable, an act which could not be forgiven. It seemed like a very reasonable option then. In fact, it seemed like the only way to recover their loss. In his desperation to make good their money, he went and bought them a penny stock. The tip was from an insider, or so his distinguished senior colleagues told him, a sure shot double if not more. That was a fortnight earlier, now that stock had lost more than half its value, and he was not even sure about its price any more.

Later that evening he would be celebrated as a survivor and made a member of the clan; but in his heart he didn't have much to cheer about. He was an outcast in his social circle and with no clients left, he didn't know how long he would last in the company either.

He was sitting there, down in the dumps when he heard a voice call out his name. At first, he thought he was imagining things, but then he heard the voice again, this time a little louder. He turned around.

It was Sunny, the bad ass CEO of his company.

Varun jumped out of his chair and stood at attention.

'Come over to my room, Varun.'

Retail Clients are Meant to be Looted

OMG! This can't be good. Several thoughts ran through Varun's mind as he hurriedly walked behind Sunny to his room. Had he done something wrong? Was he in trouble?

This wasn't the first time he was meeting Sunny. He had been to his room once before, when he had mistaken the open door for an invitation, and had walked in confidently, carrying with him his boyish charm and overconfidence. He had hoped to discuss his problems and gain some sympathy. What he had got was humiliation and abuse.

'Stop whimpering like a bitch and deal with the problem,' Sunny had yelled.

He had immediately realised his mistake and promised to never repeat it again. The door to Sunny's room was always open. He liked it that way. But it wasn't an invitation for everyone to enter. You entered that room only if you had earned it—i.e. you were a performer. If you were a loser, you didn't dare go near it. Non-performers kept away from

Sunny. Some speculated that Sunny could smell fear from a distance. In that case, he must know by now that Varun was shitting in his pants.

'Close the door behind you and take a seat,' he said.

Varun sat down but did not have the nerve to look him in the eye.

'Do we have a problem? You look worried,' he asked.

'No problem.'

'Are you sure?' he asked again.

"Is this a trap? The last time I had confessed, Sunny had thrown me out of the room, yelling 'don't come here with your problems.' No way am I going to fall for this again. I am not even sure he would want to listen, just does not seem the type. Why will he care about my moral dilemmas?"

'Nothing I can't manage,' he replied. 'I was just reflecting on the past three months, when you called me.'

'You have survived. Frankly, I didn't expect it.'

Varun smiled back.

"*Neither did I......*" But he decided to keep his thoughts to himself.

'You will not tell me your problem. That's fine by me. It seems you have learnt your lesson from our past encounter,' said Sunny with a smile.

Varun thanked his lucky stars that he hadn't given in to the desire to unburden himself again.

'Let me share a few things with you which will make you feel better. First of all, you shouldn't feel too bad about your friends and family whose money you lost.'

"Yeah! Easy for you to say, fucker. They aren't your uncles and aunts. You don't have to face them. Their words don't haunt you in the night keeping you awake. I have to listen to the taunts from my father, not you."

'Retail clients are meant to be looted. If you don't do it, someone else will. I say, better you than someone else. At least their sacrifice is not in vain. So what if they didn't make it willingly. It's helped to pull you through your probation.'

Varun looked puzzled. "*How does he know what's going on in my mind. Has one of the guys been talking to him? Could it be Anil or Devika...? Nah, they wouldn't.*"

'I don't understand,' he said. 'What do you mean?'

'Privileged information spells money in the markets. However, information availability is lopsided. It is not a level playing field.'

'Who has access to privileged information?' asked Varun.

'The research houses. They share this information selectively, first with their proprietary desks, then institutional clients and HNIs.'

'When does retail get access to this information?'

'At the fag end when no one else wants it.'

Varun nodded his head. It was making sense to him now.

'So, the retail clients are at a big disadvantage from the very beginning,' he said.

'Exactly,' Sunny animatedly affirmed.

Ordinary people are always at a disadvantage, everywhere. Take a New-Year bash at a hotel, for example. Celebrities, and rich, influential people are on the invitation list. They don't pay a penny for the invite, drink the best champagne and eat the juiciest portion of the steak. The ordinary folks on the other hand, have to buy exorbitantly priced tickets to subsidise the free booze and steaks of the celebrities. They have to line up to enter the venue, and by the time they enter, all the champagne is finished. All that remains are a few beers and some leftover meat on the bone. It is the same for retail clients who pay the highest rate of brokerage for biased, asymmetrical information which is bound to make them a loss.

'But why do they act on this information? Why not buy any of the other listed companies?'

'Good question. They get trapped because of blocking.'

'What is blocking?'

'It refers to the conditioning of the human mind. When you are bombarded repeatedly with a specific attribute of a product, you tend to overlook all other aspects and concentrate only on that particular attribute. This concept has been used by advertisers for decades to sell us products.'

'How does it apply to stock markets?'

'When these so called market experts keep harping about 20-25 stocks from morning till evening, they tend to block the retail investors from considering any of the other 10,000 shares listed on the exchanges. They act like cowboys who are essential to herd the animals into the pen. Once they have been herded, they are ready for the slaughter.'

'All these market experts are part of the game?'

'Of course, they are. They are either on the payroll of companies which want them to promote their stock, or they own shares of those companies. There are no free lunches in the stock market.'

'Bloody hell. Everything is rigged.'

'Almost everything is.'

Varun felt a little better after the pep talk. He felt a bit of the burden ease from his shoulders. What he had done didn't seem so terrible after all.

However, he wasn't smiling yet. He still didn't know how he was going to generate the revenue required to meet his target in the coming months. None of his existing clients wanted to trade. Even if they did, they didn't have the money in their account to generate any substantial revenue. He had another 35 accounts with 'nil' balance mapped to him. He wasn't sure how many of them could be converted into active traders. In all likelihood, there would be a single transaction in these accounts i.e. selling their stock options when the IPO came out. He had signed them on at an exceptionally high rate of 1 per cent brokerage to milk them on this transaction. However, this on its own would not be sufficient to meet his target. He had one more account, belonging to Aunty-ji, with an approximate stock value of Rs 1,20,000. This account was still a work in progress and was perhaps the only active account he had which could generate some revenue. However, given his past track record, he wondered how long this account would survive his onslaught.

'Still not smiling,' said Sunny. 'Wondering how you are going to get your numbers?'

"WTF?! They were right. This guy definitely has a sixth sense."

'Don't worry, you will have plenty of fodder to help you achieve your numbers. We have almost 800 unallocated clients in the system. These were opened by your ex-colleagues. Most of these clients will be allocated amongst the six of you.'

'Excuse me! But I think you mean the seven of us.'

'No! Pooja has left this group. She is joining the compliance department. I received a call from Jayant, the head of operations, earlier today, requesting her release. I am sure he influenced her. What a waste of talent. I told Pooja that she was making a big mistake. She worked hard to churn the milk and now that the time has come to eat the cream, she is leaving us.'

Varun wasn't surprised. His respect for Pooja had increased many fold. She possessed both character and integrity, something that he found increasingly lacking in himself. Pooja called a spade a spade and didn't mince her words. She was no quitter. Despite her dislike for the job, she finished her probation to the satisfaction of her manager.

'That is a big loss,' he said.

'Aaah! It is her loss. There is no comparison between us and compliance. We bring the business. They survive on our spoils and then question the manner in which we do business!'

'Anyway, coming back to our work, 750-800 accounts split between the six of you is enough fodder to keep you going till the end of the year or maybe longer.

'In addition, you all have your own 20 odd accounts. While these might be worthless for you, they are ready fodder for another relationship manager. Your existing clients don't trust you because you lost them money. All we need to do is change the relationship manager on these accounts.'

'Are you sure they will start trading merely by changing the relationship manager?'

'Yes. They have tasted blood. They might have lost money, but they recognise that there is also an opportunity to make money. If they open an account with a new broker, they will start afresh. On the other hand, if we reallocate a relationship manager who is able to convince them that the loss incurred by them was due to lack of trading skill rather than the market itself, they will believe him. It's not that they are gullible, but they want to believe him. All you need to do is acknowledge the loss. It makes them very comfortable. They think that at least this guy is not running away from his responsibility.'

'A known devil is surely better than an unknown devil,' agreed Varun. 'I wonder how many times we can reallocate relationship managers.'

'Don't be cheeky. It depends on how badly the client wishes to recover his loss. By the time he figures out that all relationship managers are nincompoops, all we need to do is send someone senior to him.

'Now go and relax. I will see you later at the party.'

Truth or Dare

Varun was amongst the last people to arrive at the party. Some relationship managers had made a dash for the venue straight after market closing. After all, booze was on tap tonight and the office was footing the bill.

It wasn't that he didn't want to come earlier. But just as he was about to leave his house, he had a showdown with his father.

'All dressed up to celebrate?' asked Mr Aggarwal, sarcastically. 'Already forgotten the pain you have inflicted on your family and friends?'

'No, I haven't. I feel guilty and live with it every day. Haven't you seen me taking the backdoor to avoid them?'

'Hiding in backdoor alleys will not make right what you have done,' replied Mr Aggarwal.

'I know, it won't. But what else can I do? I went back to ask them for more money. But they all refused. How can I recover the losses if I don't have money to trade?'

'Ha-ha! Give you more money after what you did! Even I would have declined.'

'I did lose their money. But you can't question my intent, Papa,' replied Varun. 'My conscience is clear.'

'If only you listened to me and learnt from my experience.'

'Move on! Times have changed. You can't let one incident scar you for life. I have seen many people making money on the exchange. There is a big opportunity out there. I hope someday you will appreciate my perspective.'

Those were the last words he spoke before slamming shut the front door.

"Why does he keep taunting me all the time, repeating the same thing again and again? As it is, I am going through so much stress. Doesn't he realise that he is not helping me? What does he know, doing a nine to five job? There is no gain without taking some risk. I hear what he is saying, but if the market is skewed against the retail investors, then I am fighting the system already. It can't be helped.... I can only try and at least my intentions are honourable.... Another person will take their money and lose it and not even feel bad."

The aggression in the office was rubbing off on Varun. He now reacted more often to his father's taunts. A few months earlier this would have been unimaginable. Now they had frequent showdowns.

He looked around for his friends and was pleased to see them standing in one corner. Anil already held a beer, and Pooja and Devika were having an animated discussion. What now, he wondered as he walked towards them.

'You chickened out,' said Devika, with a smile of satisfaction. 'Didn't I tell you that you were a misfit? This place is not meant for softies like you, darling.'

'She hasn't chickened out,' said Varun. 'She has gone through the same rigour as any one of us.'

'Devika, you of all the people shouldn't be questioning my hard work,' said Pooja.

'Ha-Ha! Some people work hard. Others work smart. In the end, the only thing that matters is the result,' replied Devika.

'I am proud that Pooja has the courage to speak out and stand up for what she believes in. I wonder how many of us have that kind of courage,' said Varun.

'Speak for yourself,' retorted Devika. 'I am in no mood for your lecture.'

'Come on, guys,' interrupted Anil, hoping to ease the tension. 'These bastards will finish the booze while we squabble amongst ourselves. We can have this stimulating conversation after the booze is over.'

They walked to the bar, picked up a drink each and joined a group of people playing 'Truth & Dare'. It was a simple game. People sat in a circle. A bottle lay on its side at the centre and was rotated horizontally. When the bottle stopped, the person sitting opposite the mouth of the bottle had to choose,'Truth or Dare'. If he opted for 'Truth', he could be asked any question, no matter how embarrassing, and he had to answer it. If he opted for 'Dare', he would be asked to do an activity.

The rules of the game were the same tonight, with one difference. A shot of alcohol had to be downed after each round. This was an ice breaker and ensured that people lost their inhibitions. Initially, everyone opted for truth and the questions asked were both mundane and boring. However, as the rounds progressed, the alcohol began to show effect. The questions now became bolder and some started opting for 'Dare'.

The first person amongst them to be called out was Pooja. She expectedly opted for 'Truth'.

Devika pounced on the opportunity to embarrass her and asked,' Is your love sitting amongst us?'

'Yes,' replied Pooja, without blinking an eye to roaring applause from the crowd.

A few rounds later came Devika's turn and she chose 'Dare'.

'Kiss someone amongst us,' said her ex-mentor with a sheepish smile, hoping that it would be his lucky day.

But Devika had no plans to oblige him, not just yet. She pulled Anil by his collar and gave him a hard lip lock that lasted an eternity, bruising his lips in the process. By the time it ended, the hair on Anil's nape was standing and much more. Anil was smiling with satisfaction, the flavour of mint still lingering in his mouth.

Pooja looked enormously relieved. Thank God! The recipient of the kiss had not been Varun.

Varun, however, was clearly disappointed and quickly downed another drink.

The game continued and soon it was Anil's turn. He opted for 'Dare', hoping to reciprocate Devika's affection. Sadly for him, however, he was asked to stand on a chair and do a striptease to the song 'You Sexy Thing'. He performed his act with great gusto and if his colleagues had not stopped him, he would have done a full Monty!

The game was generating such excitement that the senior members of the company, who until then had stayed at the bar, decided to join in. The stakes were significantly higher now. The game had become serious.

As it progressed, most people took the easier way out and opted for 'Truth'. Until it was Varun's turn. What would he choose, 'Truth or Dare'? Normally, Varun would have chosen 'truth'. But he was many drinks down and 'dare' seemed the braver choice.

Sunny was surprised at his choice. Was Varun challenging him? The line between bravery and stupidity was thin at the best of times, and when drunk, it became totally blurred. Varun was going to pay for his stupidity.

'You have the balls to ask for a dare,' exclaimed Sunny loudly. 'I like your guts.'

The whole room suddenly became quiet and the music sounded too loud.

'Take a 'Strongman' shot,' said Sunny. 'Let's see if you have it in you.'

Varun looked bewildered. He didn't know what a 'Strongman' shot was.

Someone ran to the bar and brought him a shot of tequila with salt and a wedge of lime.

Varun, looked at the tequila. Did they want him to have a tequila shot? What was the big deal in that?

Except, this wasn't any ordinary tequila shot. When you took a shot of tequila, you first licked the salt, then drank the tequila and finally squeezed the lemon in your mouth. In a 'Strongman' shot, you snorted the salt, drank the tequila, and finally squeezed the lemon inside your eyes.

For Sunny, this was the ultimate way to test the mettle of a person. Many had declined in the past and many others had failed.

Varun focussed on the shot of tequila in front of him. He had to do it fast, so that it was finished before the pain hit him.

He yelled aloud and the crowd cheered. Then, in a whisker, he bent down, snorted the salt into his nostrils, downed the tequila in a single gulp and squeezed the lemon into his eyes. Then he waited for the pain to hit.

In just a few seconds, he was in excruciating pain as the salt burnt through his nostrils into his sinus, the acidity of the lemon ate into his cornea, and the tequila burnt a fiery hole all the way to his stomach. His eyes went blood red and tears rolled down his cheeks. There was only one way to make this better. He took a few gulps of whisky straight from a bottle kept next to him. The ordeal ended a minute later as the alcohol numbed his senses.

He tried to focus through his blurred eyes on the cheering crowds. He was now an alpha male who had proven his mettle and earned their respect. He could do no wrong tonight. But then, the night had just begun.

When the Dog Became a Wolf

The party continued into the night, the music became louder and the human spirit wilder. Almost the entire office gyrated to Bollywood numbers, human bodies pressed against each other, trying to find space on the small dance floor. Blouse buttons had been undone and sleeves rolled up as the sweet smell of alcohol and human sweat filled the air.

The free flowing alcohol was taking its toll and several people lay passed-out on the floor, some covered in their own vomit and urine. There were bizarre scenes all over the room—a guy relieving himself against the curtains, presumably, because he thought it was the urinal; one chap lay on the floor pretending to be drunk so that he could get a glimpse of what was not on offer. The girls were so drunk that they didn't give rat's ass about him or anyone else.

Pooja stuck to Varun like a leech, not allowing any woman to come close to him. He was vulnerable tonight, for he had drunk far too much. After his 'daring' antic, there were many hungry eyes vying for his attention. She was not going to leave him alone even for a second.

Meanwhile, Anil fully exploited the opportunities that presented themselves on the dance floor, kissing and hugging every girl he could lay his hands on. His hands were like the tentacles of an octopus and he stretched them far and wide, catching unsuspecting girls, the more drunk the better.

Suddenly, some fool made a human train and ran through the middle of the dance floor pushing and trampling on people as they fell down. In the commotion that followed, Pooja got separated from Varun. As Varun struggled to find his way out of the melee, a hand pulled at his shoulder. Presuming it was Pooja, he turned around. But it was Devika, blouse buttons open, hair flowing, like a sex goddess. She looked like his fantasies come to life.

She gave him a smile full of lust. They looked at each other for a second or two, then Devika took charge. She caressed his thighs with her hands and whispered, 'How long will you keep away from me? I saw the look in your eyes when I kissed Anil. I know you want me, darling. Stop holding out, you are not a dog who can be tamed, you are a wolf. Stop babysitting Pooja and take me, before it's too late.'

"Don't do it boy. Control your base instincts. This is not you."

But her curvaceous body was pressed against his, the loud music and the alcohol in his blood made his inner voice very hard to heed. The next second they were kissing each other, their tongues fighting for dominance. One kiss led to another; their hands greedily explored each other's bodies. They passionately embraced and stumbled through the packed dance floor. Devika was on fire and bit hard on his lower lip causing it to bleed.

Varun withdrew to nurture his bruised lip, and at that moment he saw Pooja standing behind Devika, looking devastated. He didn't know what to say. But his actions had done all the talking. Devika followed his glance, turned around and saw Pooja. She didn't need to say anything either, her small triumphant smile was enough to send Pooja running off the dance floor into the lonely night.

'Oh my God! What have I done?' cried Varun.

'Stop whining,' she said. 'I didn't see any remorse when your hands were busy exploring my body. You have desired me for years and don't have the guts to admit it.'

'Take this,' she said, handing him a shot of tequila.

As he gulped it down, she slid her hands up his thighs, teasing him, playing with his manhood. She fuelled his passion and lust into a rage. He was now grunting like a wild animal. The tame dog had given way to the wild wolf.

"I have been the good boy for too long, and what do I have to show for it?".

'You will get what you desire,' he exclaimed, pulling her by her hands, half walking, half dragging her towards the exit at the other end of the room.

They were on fire as they climbed down the stairs, barely able to control their hunger. He dragged her to the dark alley behind the stairs.

'You want this, now you shall have it!' He pushed her skirt up, ripped off her panties and mounted her from the back. He thrust into her with anger and passion. She groaned as he moved faster. They made love like two animals in heat, again and again, till they were so exhausted that neither of them could stand up. They lay on the cold ground, sweat running down their bodies.

After a while, Devika got up and left without a word. Varun lay there for another few minutes, gazing into the starry night, feeling no remorse, a smile pasted on his face. He felt a sense of freedom and elation. It was a fantasy come true; the boy had become a man. He stood up and picked up the torn red panty from the ground. It was a souvenir from the night.

The ringing phone woke him the next day at noon.

'Dude, do you have any idea where I was after the party?' asked Anil.

'No clue, buddy,' he replied. 'Why? What happened?'

'I woke up this morning with a seven feet signage in my room,' replied Anil.

'Ha-Ha! What does it say?'

'Kebabs. I have no idea where it came from. It's so darn big, no way could I have carried it on my own.'

'Don't worry, buddy, we all do stupid things when we are drunk. Your signage should have a number,' said Varun.

'Yeah! It does. Thanks mate, I didn't think of that,' replied Anil. 'By the way, do you know why Pooja is so grumpy today?'

'Yeah! Maybe I do,' said Varun, pulling out the red panty from his pocket.

FINDING THEIR FEET

All it Took was a Little Nudge

The stock price of Reddy Oil & Gas had climbed over 20 per cent during the past month. All it had taken was a little nudge from Salil-bhai, to push it over the psychological mark of Rs 200. Once this level had been breached, the stock took a life of its own, reaching new highs every consecutive week.

With limited number of shares available in the market, demand outstripped supply as greedy investors chased its price to new highs. Everyone wanted a piece of the action. As predicted by Salil-bhai, Reddy's story about the turnaround in the company's fortune was readily accepted. Nobody was foolish enough to argue with the market. After all, the market was never wrong. And the rise in the stock price confirmed his story.

Salil-bhai calmly enjoyed the ride from the sidelines. He regularly analysed the *Bhav Copy*, tracking the shareholding of the company. In the beginning, 6 per cent of the free float was held by retail investors i.e. 'the weaker hands'. However, slowly 'stronger hands' began to appear in the *Bhav Copy,* signifying the transfer of shares from retail investors to institutions. He knew from past experience that as long as the shares were held by stronger hands, there would be no correction in the price of the stock. The changing shareholding reaffirmed his belief that this rally had only just begun and had a long way to go. Soon, the larger institutions, attracted by the frenzied buying, would be knocking on Reddy's door.

A week later, the company secretary of Reddy Oil & Gas received the first call from a fund house. This was followed by calls from a few other funds. Everybody wanted to meet Rajesh Reddy, the face of the company.

The fund managers met with Reddy one after another. They came with their homework done and numbers at their fingertips. But numbers meant very little in today's world, as one scam after another had taught them. They could be easily manipulated and were often misleading. What they really wanted to know was if the share price of Reddy Oil & Gas would rise in the future. Did Reddy value his company? Did he have the right intention? If so, was he willing to do all that was required to ensure that he didn't default on the FCCBs? Hence, after asking a few mundane questions to break the ice, they tempted him.

'Reddy sahib, I like your company,' said one of them. 'But our fund is large and any investment less than 8-10 per cent of your share capital wouldn't be worth my time. We are willing to pay a premium, if required, to acquire that.'

They all asked the same question; only the quantity of shares required changed, depending upon the size of the fund.

But Reddy wasn't tempted by their offer. He just didn't have the damn shares to spare.

'I am sorry,' he replied. 'I can't give any guarantees. You will have to purchase them from the market.'

Reddy didn't know it, but he had just given the perfect reply to satisfy all their queries.

Based on his reply, they deduced that there was very little free float available in the market, as most shares had been cornered by the stronger hands. The promoter valued his company higher than indicated by the current price in the market. This implied that he was reasonably confident of meeting the terms of conversion of the FCCBs. This was also borne out by the fact that he had increased his official holding in the company.

So it seemed that this share was definitely headed beyond Rs 450, the price at which the FCCB holders had the option to convert their bonds into equity.

Aunty-ji and Baba-ji, the Story of Your Life

Varun and Anil excitedly exchanged their visiting cards, giggling like teenage boys. They were now relationship managers, the most abused designation in the financial services industry. Almost anybody who could sell anything was called a relationship manager. Nevertheless, they had survived the tough probation and they were proud of having reached their new status.

Anil immediately exploited it by extending his terms of credit with his *cigarettewallahs*. Varun proudly gave his father his visiting card. But his father, was not impressed and gave him a sermon instead.

"Why the hell did I show him the card? He is never going to be happy at my success..."

'Organisations with substance don't need a marketing card and those with emphasis on marketing have little substance,' he had said.

Anil and Varun were still busy exchanging notes about the party when Devika arrived.

'Hello darling,' she said giving Varun a peck on the cheek.

Varun blushed deeply. He wasn't used to public display of affection.

'Don't be shy, baby,' she said looking at him.

'What about me?' asked Anil looking at her expectantly. 'Where is my kiss?'

'You got lucky last week,' she replied. 'Don't make it a habit.'

'But that wasn't just a kiss,' retorted Anil.

'That was the trailer, darling,' she replied. 'Varun enjoyed the movie.'

Anil turned to Varun as soon as Devika left the scene.

'Dude, do we have some catching up to do?'

'Yeah,' replied Varun. 'Let's go down for a smoke.'

'What have you been up to? Why didn't you tell me earlier?'

'You were too preoccupied with that signage. I didn't want to add to your troubles.'

'That's bullshit and you know it. Come on, give me the details; tell me everything.'

'Nothing, dude. I got frisky with her on Friday night.'

'Don't sound so modest idiot, tell me all. Did you hit first base?'

Varun made a hand gesture that implied the question was irrelevant.

'How stupid of me! Of course you did. But how about second base?'

Anil was now giggling with excitement.

Varun raised his eyebrows.

'Third base? Did you go all the way?' cried Anil.

'Shhhhh...please be quiet, dude. Everyone is looking at us.'

'I don't give a shit. Answer my question!'

Varun didn't need to answer his question. The smile on his face did all the talking.

'Holy shit! You lucky son of a bitch!' said Anil. 'I am such an asshole.'

'Why?' asked Varun.

'If I had paid more attention to her that night, it could very well have been me instead of you.'

'Ha-Ha! Now you are dreaming buddy.'

'Maybe I am. But then, that's what dreams are for—imagining the impossible!

'Where was Pooja when all this was happening?'

'She was right there,' said Varun looking embarrassed. 'She saw me kissing and groping Devika on the dance floor.'

'Oh my God!'

'I didn't mean to hurt her. But you know, I have always had a thing for Devika and just couldn't control myself.'

'That's why she is pissed off,' said Anil. 'Don't worry, it had to happen, the sooner the better.'

'Yeah! I guess so,' Varun replied, a little surprised at his own lack of guilt.

He looked at his watch and said, 'Buddy, I better be leaving now. 'I have a client meeting. She must be waiting.'

'*Waah Beta*! Such urgency to meet a woman client.'

'No, boss! Nothing like that. I am meeting Aunty-ji. I had spoken about her to you earlier. Don't you remember?'

'Ok. How about catching up tomorrow evening?'

'Sorry, dude! But I am catching up with Tiwari-ji.'

'Ha-Ha! Aunty and Baba-ji, that's the story of your life, dude. I am still shocked that you managed to get Devika.'

"You wouldn't have said this had you seen me in my elements that night."

'Every dog has his day,' he said aloud. 'You will have yours soon.'

Varun rushed to Aunty's house. He found her pacing in her living room. He felt sorry for her. He had promised to call her within a week. Instead, a whole month had passed by. But what could he do? He had been so engrossed in trying to generate revenue that he hadn't had time to breathe, forget visit anyone.

"Every cloud has a silver lining. Thank God I didn't visit her earlier! Otherwise, she might have met the same fate as many of my other clients."

'Hello, Aunty-ji. How are you?'

'I am fine, Varun *beta,*' she replied. 'You must be tired. Sit and I will get some tea for you.'

There wasn't an iota of anger or disappointment in her voice. Life had not been fair to this old, childless widow. She had often received mistreatment and ridicule at the hands of society. Consequently, she had very little expectation from her fellow human beings. Any gesture of kindness, however small, was enough to melt her heart.

She was soon back with a cup of tea and Varun apologised to her.

'I am sorry it took me so long to come back with information for you.'

He handed her the pile of share certificates and said, 'These are all worthless.'

'Oh! I had hoped for better luck,' she replied.

'However, not all is lost Aunty-ji. This certificate of 100 shares of Intotys is worth Rs 1,20,000,' replied Varun.

'Wow! Rs 1,20,000,' she said, running inside the kitchen to fetch a bowl of sweets. 'This is the best news I have heard in months.'

Her joy made Varun feel good about himself, even though he was merely a courier boy who had delivered the good news to her.

'I need a few documents to get these shares transferred to your name,' said Varun, getting up with a sweet in his hand. 'I have another meeting and better be leaving now.'

'Don't worry, *beta*,' she replied. 'I shall wait for the list of documents.'

Varun was in a good mood for the remainder of the day. He somehow felt responsible for bringing a smile to Aunty-ji's face. He didn't know it yet, but life was only going to get better.

The Power of Compounding

It was 7.00 pm by the time Varun reached the bar. He found Tiwari-ji sitting at a high table, savouring a cold glass of beer.

'Am I late?' he asked.

'Nah, you are fine,' replied Tiwari-ji. 'I arrived five minutes early and took the liberty of ordering drinks.'

'Cheers,' said Varun, settling down on the chair beside him and raising his glass of beer. 'How are you?'

'I am the same old *Mullah ki daud masjid tak*. But you seem to be on a roll.'

'Ha-Ha! The alcohol went to my head the other night,' replied Varun smiling. 'Otherwise, only a fool would have accepted a challenge from Sunny.'

'I am happy that you realise that. Because Sunny never forgets nor forgives.'

'Am I in trouble?'

'Not at all. Had you failed, you would certainly have been. But you came out a winner that night and we worship winners at TBB. I think you are in his good books now.'

'Good books? How does that change my life?' asked Varun.

'It could, if you are willing to become his stooge and agree with whatever he says or does.'

'His lap dog you mean?' said Varun, agitated.

'Don't get worked up. Think about it. It will lead you to many good opportunities.'

'There is nothing to think about. I am nobody's lap dog.'

'Good to hear that. But know this, most others would have agreed.'

'I don't care. I live my life on my terms.'

They gossiped like long lost friends, Varun filling Tiwari-ji in on the happenings of the prior month—how he had been forced to dance to the tune of the market, breaking every rule of trading and losing money in the process for his family and friends.

Tiwari-ji listened calmly, with an amused smile.

'You don't look surprised!' he said.

'Yes, I am not surprised. You are not the only one, it happens with everybody. Learning in a controlled environment can never prepare you for the real thing. I am reminded of this dialogue from a Bruce Lee movie, *Bricks Don't Hit Back*. Target practice at a shooting range is very different from firing in a real life situation.'

'But why such a marked difference in performance?'

'Performance depends upon skill and control over the mind. Based on what you have told me, you couldn't handle the pressure,' said Tiwari-ji.

'How does one control the mind?'

'It will come to you with experience.'

Varun was still mulling over this, when Tiwari-ji called out excitedly.

'Hello, Sir! What are you doing here?'

Varun turned around and saw a bespectacled man, old in age but not in posture, with a firm strong voice and a glowing skin, the kind you see in those who age gracefully. He wore a Rolex on his left wrist and a Montblanc pen peeped from his top pocket.

Tiwari-ji quickly stood up and touched his feet.

'Varun, meet my guru, Mr Taneja,' he said. 'Whatever I know about the stock markets is because of him.'

Tiwari-ji had many uncles and aunts, but very few gurus. He used the words uncle and aunty liberally to describe any retail client. However, guru was reserved for high net worth clients only. This old man certainly fit the bill.

Varun shook Taneja's hand and invited him to join them for a drink.

'Sir, would you be kind enough to tell us that story about IPC?' requested Tiwari-ji.

'But you have heard it so many times,' replied Taneja.

'It is so inspiring. One more time wouldn't hurt, for the benefit of this poor soul.'

Tiwari-ji was a master at cajoling his clients. He knew that Taneja loved to tell his story.

So began the story of IPC. Taneja had taken early retirement from a sugar mill in 1988 and as part of his retirement package, received Rs 2,50,000.

'Only Rs 2,50,000?' asked Varun innocently, the memory of nearly Rs 600,000 he had lost in the previous month still fresh in his mind.

'Oh! Rs 2,50,000 was a lot of money in those days. You could buy a month's ration for two or three hundred bucks.'

He decided to invest Rs 1,50,000 in fixed deposits and the remainder in a stock. The question was, which stock should he buy?

'Do you smoke?' he asked.

'Yes, sir,' replied Varun.

'Then you will appreciate what I am going to say next.'

'Smokers are loyal to the brand of cigarette they smoke.'

Varun nodded in agreement.

Tiwari-ji had always smoked the '*OP*' brand of cigarettes and looked mildly amused. For the uninitiated, '*OP*' stood for the other person's brand. He had never purchased a packet of cigarettes in his entire life, always bumming sticks from his colleagues. His taste was more 'acquired'. It varied from day to day, depending upon the taste of the person from whom he had bummed the cigarettes.

'I smoke only IPC cigarettes and had seen their price increase manifold over time. It didn't matter how expensive they became, I never changed either the brand or the quantity I bought. This realisation was all I needed.'

Varun also smoked IPC. However, he had never given it much thought. Taneja's story was a revelation for him. The best investment decisions were often based on simple logic.

'Accordingly, I invested Rs 1,00,000 in IPC.'

'Now the story gets really interesting,' said Tiwari-ji. 'Go ahead, ask him how much it's worth today.'

'How has the stock done for you, Mr Taneja?' asked Varun.

'It's been a great journey. They kept giving dividends and bonus shares regularly. Also, the share was split a few years back. Consequently, the quantity of shares in my possession kept compounding.'

'How much is it worth today?' he asked again, no longer able to control his excitement.

'I received almost Rs 2.5 crores as dividend income.'

'Wow!'

'That's not all. Today the shares are worth another Rs 25 crores.'

Tiwari-ji whistled aloud.

'Sir, they were worth a little less the last time you narrated the story,' he said. 'Perhaps, it is time for me to collect a cheque from you again.'

They all laughed aloud. Varun asked Tiwari-ji, 'What is the face value of Intotys Technologies Ltd?'

'You mean Intotys Limited,' replied Tiwari-ji. 'I think it is Rs 5. Why do you ask?'

Varun recalled the share certificate kept at his house. It read 100 shares of Intotys Technologies Ltd with a face value of Rs 10 each. He slowly climbed down from the bar stool, shaking Mr Taneja's hand and thanking him for the story. Then he looked at Tiwari-ji and said, 'I need to hurry back home.'

'What's happened?' asked Tiwari-ji. 'Is everything alright?'

Varun only said as he rushed towards the exit, 'Taneja sahib, you might have just helped me unravel a gold mine.'

When Gourd Tasted Delicious

Varun was panting as he entered his house. He had jogged back home from the metro station. His father was watching the evening news and his mother was cooking in the kitchen. It was only 8.30 pm, and dinner was still an hour away.

He walked into the kitchen, carefully avoiding his father. He was feeling cheerful and had no intention of spoiling his mood by risking a squabbling match with him.

'Ma, I have some important work to finish,' he said. 'I will join you both for dinner after a while.'

He quietly went into his room and locked the door behind him.

Despite his efforts, however, his father had seen him.

'Your prodigal son is drunk. I can smell his foul breath till here. What kind of work does he do that he needs to lock his room?'

Varun smiled. His father was so predictable.

'No way am I going to respond and make your day,' he mumbled to himself.

He quickly pulled out the share certificate kept inside his briefcase and examined it carefully. He was right. It was dated early 1994, and mentioned 100 shares of Intotys Technologies Ltd with a face value of Rs 10 each.

He turned on his computer and opened the website of the stock exchange. The internet connection was slow. He cursed the service provider and waited impatiently for the desired page to open.

When it finally opened, he quickly typed Intotys Technologies Ltd in the search bar and waited for the results. There seemed to be some error. He typed 'Intotys Limited' this time and again pressed 'Enter'. Bingo! He was directed to the home page of Intotys Limited. He clicked on the link dealing with corporate actions. A submenu appeared showing different subheadings like dividends, rights, splits and bonus.

He clicked on 'Splits'. After a moment's notice the desired page opened. Tiwari-ji was correct, in late 1999 and early 2000, the shares of

Intotys Limited had been split and consequently the face value of the share had reduced from Rs 10 to Rs 5. So far so good.

His heart started beating faster as he navigated back to the main page and clicked on 'Bonus'. The page opened slowly, testing his patience. But what he saw blew his mind away. He quickly started scribbling on a piece of paper kept next to him.

1:1 Bonus issue in the year 1994. Total shares held 200.

1:1 Bonus issue in the year 1997. Total shares held 400.

1:1 Bonus issue in the year 1999. Total shares held 800.

Split in Face Value from Rs 10 to Rs 5 in late 1999-2000. Total shares held 1600.

As the number of shares increased, so did his level of excitement. His mind raced in the background, simultaneously calculating the value of the shares.

3:1 Bonus issue in the year 2004. Total shares held 2133.

1:1 Bonus issue in the year 2006. Total shares held 4266.

1:1 Bonus issue in the year 2011. Total shares held 8532.

1:1 Bonus issue in the year 2012. Total shares held 17064.

By the time he scribbled down the final number of 17,064 shares on the piece of paper, his heart was pounding, threatening to explode in sheer excitement. He sat back for a moment and gathered together his thoughts, his eyes transfixed on the piece of paper in front of him.

His first sense was that of complete disbelief.

"I must have made a mistake. I have had too much beer! This number just can't be true. Luck only favours the rich. And really, I have never been this lucky."

He quickly went through the scribbled notes again, re-analysing the numbers to pick out any mistake that he might have made. But there was none.

As the enormity of the number finally settled in his mind, he said out loud, 'Oh My God! 17,064!'

His father immediately retorted, 'Bloody drunk! That better not be your mobile bill.'

'Are you alright?' his mother called out from the kitchen.

'Yeah! I am fine. Never been better.'

He quickly looked at the share price of Intotys. It had closed at a high of Rs 1200 for the day. He did the maths, 17,064 shares, Rs 1200 a share, Rs 2,04,76,800.

Bloody hell! He had never seen so much money in his life. What will Aunty-ji do with so much money? He started day dreaming, his mouth salivating at the thought.

'No more samosas or Indian sweets for me. From now on, I only want to eat patties and pastries from Wengers. Also, a cold coffee from Depaul's will do just fine.'

Suddenly, his expression changed and he looked worried.

"What if she goes bonkers? It happens with age. A living example is sitting in the living room at this very moment watching the idiot box. The old man hasn't even got money and is still losing his sanity every passing day."

Or even worse, what if she has a heart attack when she hears the good news?

"I better be very careful. I should break the news to her in parts, giving her time to absorb it slowly."

In any case, there was no point in any discussion till the shares actually arrived in her account. Just in case he had made a mistake.

"Imagine the emotional roller coaster, if you are told one moment that you are a multi-millionaire, only to be told in the next that it was all a big mistake. She would certainly die on me if this were to happen."

He was still enjoying the taste of the imaginary patty in his mouth when his father's voice brought him unceremoniously back to reality. Apparently he had been speaking his thoughts aloud all this time.

'*Oye hero*! Your old man might be bonkers but he isn't deaf yet. Stop day dreaming about patties and pastries. Come out and eat the *kaddu* (gourd) that your mother has cooked for you.'

'Give me 10 minutes,' he yelled back.

He went back to calculating the numbers in his head again. If he sold the shares, he would make brokerage income of a little over

Rs 2,00,000. Enough to keep his boss at bay for a few months. This would give him enough breathing space to re-organise himself and open new accounts. Who knew, if luck favoured him then some of the accounts at the PSU might also turn out to be HNIs.

For the first time, he found himself in a comfortable situation.

But something was pricking his conscience. He had opened Aunty-ji's account at a special brokerage rate of 1 per cent, much higher than that of other regular clients. This rate was justified given the quantum of work required to bring it to completion.

However, the scenario had changed completely now. With over Rs 20,000,000 of stocks in the account, such a high rate of brokerage was sacrilege. If anyone found out, they would say that he was swindling her. Well, swindling was too harsh a word, but he was definitely taking advantage of her.

For a brief moment, he thought of reducing the rate of brokerage. But he remembered the awful pressure cooker environment in his office, his boss constantly breathing down his neck, abusing him for non-performance.

He concluded that Aunty-ji wouldn't mind indulging him a little. After all, if it wasn't for him, these riches would have never seen the light of the day.

"I will be the son that she never had. I am being so nice to her and doing all this work."

With a smile, he went off to eat the *kaddu* that his mother had prepared for him.

Even insipid bottle gourd tasted delicious tonight.

The Four-Point Formula

The next day Varun reached office earlier than usual so that he could finish the formalities required for the share transfer into Aunty-ji's account, before he started regular office work. If he could courier the application by the end of day, the shares would probably be transferred by the middle of next month, provided the application was complete in all aspects.

In the interim, he would concentrate on the accounts of the PSU. The IPO was scheduled in a week and the shares would be listed by the end of the month. These accounts were his blood line for meeting his numbers in the current month.

He typed a letter addressed to the registrar of shares attaching the share certificate along with a copy of his uncle's death certificate and details of the depository account. He put the entire set inside an envelope and asked the branch assistant to ensure that it was sent by the afternoon courier.

He returned to his seat and opened his email looking for the one containing re-allocation of clients. It was expected any time. These accounts were opened by relationship managers who had since quit the organisation. He hoped that these accounts were in better shape than the six accounts he had earmarked for re-allocation to other relationship managers.

These six accounts had been active in the prior month. But today, they were burnt beyond recognition, having lost almost their entire margin money. These clients despised him, refusing to speak with him anymore. He was happy to get rid of them. He felt sorry for the relationship managers to whom these accounts would be re-allocated and who would now have to face these clients' ire.

After deleting half a dozen spam mails, including marriage proposals from girls he didn't know, loan approvals for which he hadn't applied, he finally got to the email that he had been waiting for. He quickly opened the attachment to see the number of clients allocated to him.

Only 50 clients? What the hell? This was a far cry from the number that Sunny had mentioned the prior week. He cursed, 'The bastards must have kept the good accounts with themselves.'

'I heard that,' said his sales manager.

'You were meant to,' he yelled back.

His intuition was correct. They had kept the big clients for the experienced relationship managers. This was business after all and not charity. Experienced relationship managers were more efficient at converting client funds into brokerage income, an art which was yet to be mastered by the new kids on the block like him.

He analysed the clients allocated to him in greater detail. On an average, almost every client had lost between 60 per cent to 80 per cent of his margin money. Also, not a single client had opened the account with more than Rs 1,00,000 margin money. This implied that most of them were retail clients and the probability of finding an HNI client was small. Unless, the erstwhile relationship managers had failed to recognise the true potential of the client, being happy with Rs 1,00,000 cheque when they could have easily walked away with a much larger sum. He hoped that this was the case.

He was still analysing the list, when he heard the footsteps of his sales manager. The son of a bitch always kept such a close eye on him, that Varun heard his voice even in his sleep.

'Yes boss! What is it?' he asked.

'Don't show me attitude, shit face. You have the month to work on this client list. On the first of next month, I will ask you to return 10 clients to me. Do you understand?

'Very clearly,' replied Varun.

This was a clever way to ensure that every relationship manager diligently worked on the clients allocated to him. He heard his boss, boasting in the background about how he had to fight for these meaty accounts to be allocated to his team.

'You are lucky to get these accounts,' he said. 'They are the best of the lot. I want to see improved numbers next month.'

'Meaty, my ass,' whispered Varun.

He knew that his boss was bullshitting. No one had the balls to speak out in front of Sunny, let alone argue with him. He must have sat there trembling in a corner, hoping that he wasn't noticed.

Enough of this bullshit. Time to get some fresh air. Varun went outside looking for Tiwari-ji. He wanted to seek his advice on how to approach clients for fresh margin money. As expected, Tiwari-ji was standing next to the cigarette shop, smoking a cigarette which probably belonged to somebody else.

'What happened yesterday?' he asked. 'You left in a hurry?'

'Something is cooking up,' replied Varun. 'It's still work in progress. But tell me Dada, did you manage to get money out of Taneja?'

'Of course, I did. I had to recover the cost of the beer! Last time he narrated the story, the value of the shares was Rs 23 crores. Yesterday, he said Rs 25 crores. I immediately got a cheque of Rs 10 lakhs signed from him.'

'Ha-Ha! You are great. Always on the lookout for opportunities to exploit.'

'Enough about me. What brings you here?'

'I have been allocated a few clients. How should I approach them for additional margin money?'

'If you were a beautiful woman, I would have said that a smile is all you need.'

'Come on boss, don't bullshit with me.'

'No! I am serious, Varun. These oldies don't know how to handle women. Their knees begin to tremble upon seeing a beautiful woman.'

'I guess that's why Devika does such brisk business.'

Your friend Devika? Varun, even my knees begin to tremble when I see her.'

'Boss, stop joking around. What will work for me?'

'Your problem is that you aren't even a networker.'

'I don't agree. I can network.'

'You are not getting my point. You aren't a natural storyteller. You have formal relationships with your clients. You visit them only for work. My clients are like my drinking buddies. I can take liberties with them. Uncle, I am short on my targets, give me some money. You could never do this. Even if you did, you wouldn't get a penny from them.'

'I think you have only one choice. The four point formula.'

'What is that?'

'Point One—empathise with your client. Feel his pain. He will cry his heart out and you need to rub Iodex on his injury.

'Point Two—make sure that you abuse the shit out of his erstwhile relationship manager. Hold the son of a bitch responsible for everything wrong with the client. If he doesn't have a pretty wife, that too is the relationship manager's fault.'

'Abuse? Are you sure?'

'Oh yes! Clients love it. Don't be embarrassed, go all out and abuse the previous relationship manager.

'Point Three—convince the client that you can make money for him. 'By God! I will make good your loss.'

'Boss, with my exemplary track record, how am I supposed to convince the clients that I shall make money for him?'

'Varun, the client doesn't know that you know nothing. Go to that Gupta fellow in the Branch back office. Ask him to hand you ledgers of a few clients who have made money. Gupta knows what needs to be done. He always keeps a few ledgers in his drawer for fellows like you.'

'We actually have some clients who have made good money in the markets?'

'Of course, we do. Mind you, we have nothing to do with it. These clients work independently, on their own information and skills, making money despite their relationship managers. This is our little secret, but then your client doesn't know that.'

'Just show him the ledger and don't blabber. Let the ledger do the talking. He will be convinced that you can make money for him.'

'As soon as you feel that he has taken the bait, Point Four—give him a jolt. "Sir, how can I recover your loss if I don't have money to invest? There is little money left in your account and if I have to recover your losses, I will need some more." The moment you get the cheque in your hand, make a dash for the main gate.'

'Why is that?'

'Otherwise, you will give the client an opportunity to start asking difficult questions, like how do you propose to recover his loss, what will be your action plan and so on. So, take the cheque and run.'

It's Child's Play for Me

It was extremely difficult to maintain a long face without any corresponding feeling of remorse. But this was exactly what was required, as Varun listened intently to the sobbing old man.

The slightest hint of a smile would have ruined the performance. But Varun was a perfectionist and had practised this act several times in front of a mirror. There seemed to be no doubt that he was in grief. The only thing missing were a few tears.

Anil had offered him a bottle of Vicks Vaporub, which if applied under his eyes would have let loose a river of sorrows. But he had politely declined. This was too melodramatic even for his sensibilities.

He anxiously waited for the tirade to end so that he could move to the next stage of his act. However, his client was unrelenting in his onslaught, partly, because he had lost over 80 per cent of his money and also because he was old and lonely and needed this opportunity to talk to someone.

Varun looked at his watch. He had been listening quietly for 45 minutes and was losing patience.

And just then, his prayers were answered as the old man choked, his mouth dry with all the ranting. Varun quickly passed him a glass of water before he died on him. This was the opening he was waiting for, it was time to make the old man his father. He took charge.

'Uncle, you have clearly been wronged. I am shocked. You are like my father. I feel for you. How could someone do this to you?'

The father remark seemed to have had the desired effect and the old man now listened intently to him.

'Your old relationship manager was a bastard. The son of a bitch will definitely go to hell.'

The old man flinched at this and looked startled. The curse words made him uncomfortable.

'Uncle, you should consider yourself lucky.'

The old man looked surprised.

'Don't get me wrong. I am not trying to undermine what happened to you. But I have heard such horror stories about your relationship manager. I met this gentleman who lost his entire retirement pension. Can you believe it, an old man like yourself losing his entire life's savings?'

'Oh my god!' exclaimed the old man.

'We fired the bastard as soon as we received the first complaint. Unfortunately, the damage had already been done. But don't worry uncle. You are in safe hands now.'

'This loss can be recovered. It will take some time, but it can certainly be done.'

'But how son?'

'Uncle! Leave that to me. This is what I do for a living.'

"Crorepati ko lakhpati, lakhpati ko kangaal, jawaan ko buddhaa bana doon, main hun Varun Aggarwal."

(I convert a billionaire to a millionaire, a millionaire to a pauper, a youth to an old man, I am Varun Aggarwal)

'You just concentrate on your morning walks and let me worry about these money matters.'

Varun pulled out the ledgers of the two clients from his bag.

'Uncle, look at this client: I doubled his money last year. Or, look at this guy: over 40 per cent return in three months.'

The old man looked at the ledgers for a minute. Handing them back to Varun, he said, 'I can't understand these.'

Varun tried explaining them for a few minutes, until he realised that the problem lay elsewhere.

'You can't see well, Uncle, so I can't show you.'

'I believe you, son,' he said. 'I don't need to see these. But the big question is, can you recover my loss?'

'It's child's play for me, Uncle. Of course I can recover your loss. But given your risk profile, I need to be extra cautious. I cannot be aggressive as you have already lost a lot of money.'

'I don't want any extra returns son, I just want back my hard earned money.'

'I understand, uncle. But you will have to help me out a little here.'

'What do you want?'

'Uncle, there is only Rs 15,000 left in your account. Suppose, I do an exceptional job and am able to double your money. Even then it would only amount to Rs 30,000, a long way from the Rs 1,00,000 that you had started with.'

'To recover your loss, I need some more money. I don't want to sell you a dream which cannot be realised.'

'How much more money do you want?'

'Another Rs 75,000 should suffice.'

Two minutes later, Varun was filling in the requisite details in the cheque book. The old man's hands trembled as he put his signature on the cheque.

As soon as the cheque was signed, Varun got up to leave.

"Time to make a quick escape, before the tape recorder starts again."

What if the old man asked him how he intended to recover his loss?

Stock Manipulation—An Easy Game

Salil-bhai had the largest non-promoter holding in Reddy Oil & Gas. If only the free float was considered, then his position was the largest, even larger than that of Reddy. However, since this position was split between several *benaami* companies, it wasn't consolidated in the *Bhav Copy*.

A large position meant that Salil-bhai was always the counter party to the rest of the market. He was buying when others were selling, and selling when others were buying. However, this had to be done intelligently to ensure that he retained control over the stock.

The stock of Reddy Oil & Gas had rallied one way from Rs 200 to Rs 300 without taking a breather. During this run, Salil-bhai had been selling small quantities of shares to test the strength of the market. Over the last fortnight, he had found the resolve of the market wanting. The rally was showing signs of fatigue.

He had to act before the others. And, he had to do so forcefully. Only then would his actions dictate the trend in the market. He perused the *Bhav Copy* one last time, analysing the changing shareholding of the company. Was there any pent up demand from the institutions? He didn't want to sell if they were still buying. Otherwise, they would simply absorb his shares. He was relieved to find that they had stopped buying ever since the price of the share crossed Rs 250. It was time to sell.

He sold mercilessly, not giving any market participant an opportunity to act. The stock crashed to Rs 270 within two days setting panic amongst the traders and retail investors. They didn't have the belly to take such volatility and threw in their towels. Salil-bhai started buying again, but slowly, allowing the stock to decline further. As it moved within kissing distance of Rs 250, he started buying aggressively. He wasn't going to make it easy for the institutions. He wanted to tease them. He wanted them to chase the stock.

And chase they did, driving the price of Reddy Oil & Gas above its previous high of Rs 300. This time the momentum was strong and there was no stopping it. Traders and retail investors who had sold their stock at lower levels scrambled to board the bandwagon again. Salil-bhai didn't need to add any fuel to the fire and sat on the sidelines waiting for the next opportunity to intervene.

By selling at the top and covering his position at lower prices, he was able to lower his cost of acquisition. While the stock of Reddy Oil & Gas continued steady in a broad uptrend, there were several counter cycles. Each time Salil-bhai sold mercilessly only to buy back at a lower price, thus lowering his cost of acquisition. Also, by ensuring timely corrections in the stock price, he made sure that the rally in the stock remained stable.

Master Pinto and Rani Laxmi Bai

It was like any other day when Varun reached the office. He didn't pay much attention to the lady–a visitor–waiting in the reception area. He heard her asking for Pinto, one of the relationship managers.

Pinto was a sweet chap, but he could not handle the pressure and had quit a few days earlier. Varun had been surprised that he had survived this long.

The lady was surprised when she was informed that Pinto had left the organisation.

'Oh! When did he leave?' she asked.

'Madam, only a few days back,' replied the receptionist.

'Oh! No wonder he hasn't been answering my calls. Can I meet somebody who can run me through my stock holding statement?'

'Sure! Madam,' replied the receptionist. 'I will direct you to the branch back office person.'

The back office person looked baffled as he handed over the stock holding statement to the lady. The statement didn't contain any stock holdings.

'This statement is not correct,' replied the lady.

The poor fellow refreshed the system and checked the records again hoping that the results would change. But the statement still showed a 'Nil' holding.

Looking a little worried, he asked, 'Madam, do you remember what you had purchased?'

'Of course I remember,' she replied. 'I had purchased what you call them, 'options' two months earlier.'

His face went pale. This matter was way above his pay grade to handle. He immediately took her to the branch manager's office, relieved that he didn't have to be the one to tell her that her options had expired and she had lost her money in the process.

And then the shit hit the fan.

Apparently, Pinto wasn't as sweet as he appeared to be. He had met this middle class lady a few months earlier and convinced her to part with a portion of her husband's money. 'Madam, I will make you so much money that you will join two more "kitties",' he said to her.

Excited at the prospect of being part of three kitty groups, the lady parted with her husband's hard earned money, knowing well that he would not approve of her dabbling in the stock markets. So far so good—Pinto had been creative and had shown ingenuity by enticing the lady with exaggerated returns.

But then, Master Pinto made her buy index options on the Nifty. Consequently, a housewife who had no clue about stock markets, was now dabbling in options, a product meant for professional traders.

Options, unlike stocks, expired on the last Thursday of the month. Hence, depending on how the trade went, you either made money or lost it all. But Pinto forgot to convey this critical information to the lady. Perhaps, because he didn't consider it relevant, but most probably because it was inconvenient.

He survived another month by making this lady his sacrificial goat. The said options expired on the last Thursday of the month and all her money was lost. But she had no clue. From time to time she would call up Pinto, who would feed her some cock and bull story. Then one day, Pinto stopped taking her calls. She kept trying to reach him for a few more days. Finally, she landed up at the office demanding to see her stock holding statement.

Everyone dived for cover that day. You could hear her loud, angry voice even in the trading room. She refused to leave the reception. Varun had only read about Rani Laxmi Bai in history books but this woman seemed to be a real life version of the ferocious lady! She would not budge until Sunny intervened with some spiel and handed her over to Tiwari-ji, the snake charmer of the office.

Tiwari-ji kept playing the flute as long as she was agitated, listening patiently to her as she vented her ire. As one cup of tea followed another, she slowly calmed down, tired out from her rage and agitation.

Once she was calm and composed, Tiwari-ji simply told her the truth.

'Madam, you have been taken on a wild ride,' he said. 'My sympathies are with you, but you must recognise that you are also at fault. Didn't you make the trades?' he asked.

'But I didn't know what they were.'

'All the more reason you shouldn't have indulged in them. He took you on a wild goose chase and you agreed to go along.'

She had nothing to say to this and was soon nodding her head in agreement.

'Madam, Pinto the magician has vanished and I don't have a magic wand to deliver the returns he promised,' said Tiwari-ji. 'However, if we invest diligently, good returns can be generated.'

Ten minutes later they were chatting like long lost friends, discussing the future course of action. Before she left, she gave him a cheque for margin money.

WALK IN THE CLOUDS

The Devil Called Sales

It was the beginning of November. There was a nip in the air and the first signs of approaching winter were visible. Varun, Anil, Devika and Pooja had all been confirmed and had found their bearings. They had adapted to the office environment.

However, the pressure was continuous. They were still abused regularly by their superiors to deliver on unachievable targets. But unlike in the past, there was no fear of losing their jobs. They now understood the liberties they could take based on their performance.

Life was never easy in sales. The sooner one realised this, the faster one adjusted and adapted. It didn't matter how many accounts were opened, how much margin money was collected or revenue generated by a relationship manager, the organisation always wanted more. This was the devil called sales.

It is important in sales to figure out how one's performance measures vis-à-vis others, where one stands in the scheme of things. This is essential, because the boss seldom appreciates one's work. At best, he will take one out for a few beers, and just when one has relaxed, whisper the revised targets.

However, at TBB, if the motivation was money, then there was no better job than sales. There was no limit on how well one could do, or how much one could earn.

Devika made incentives every month. She knew her strengths, and was a master at exploiting and manipulating people around her to meet her goals. She always enjoyed a rather–to put it politely–warm relationship with her bosses. She played the music and they danced to her tunes. She was always able to find helping hands willing to assist her in her endeavours. There were relationship managers who not only parted with their clients in her favour, but also took on the onus of generating revenue in those accounts. All this for some friendly laughter and casual flirting.

When it came to collecting money from clients, Devika didn't need anyone. She was in a league of her own, the most successful amongst the three of them. She had both charm and class, which wasn't an area of strength for either Varun or Anil.

When visiting a new client, she broke the ice by engaging in chirpy, lively chatter and casual flirting. Once they relaxed and started enjoying her presence, she gradually manoeuvred the discussion to the inhospitable work environment prevalent in her office, how she was constantly hounded by her supervisors to deliver on numbers. Soon, they were feeling sorry for her and that is when she innocently asked a rather unassuming question, putting them on the spot in the process.

'Sir, you wouldn't allow me to return to the office without a cheque, would you?'

By this time, even the most experienced clients were taken in by her charm and innocence. Consequently, she always walked out of these meetings with a cheque in her hand.

However, her act would change if she was visiting a client whose account had been reallocated to her. In such a situation, she would sit silently in front of the client with sad, dopy eyes. After a few minutes, she would request them in a soft voice to abuse her and take out their anger.

'All I have heard since morning is hatred and anger for no fault of mine.'

She was now the epitome of sorrow. Her expressions would suggest that she was going to break down at any moment. This act was so realistic that most clients wanted to help this poor soul, who was at the receiving end for no fault of hers. Soon, they would be on the same side abusing a common enemy, the erstwhile relationship manager. A little later, the client would sign a cheque to help her out of her misery. Not a word was ever discussed about stock markets and returns in these meetings.

Life in office couldn't have been better for Varun. He was also consistently making incentives month on month. However, unlike Devika, his performance was largely dependent on a single account, that belonging to his favourite aunty. Oh yes! The old woman was now his favourite aunty.

The recognition that came from qualifying for incentives together with greed for money had taken him over. Consequently, despite the fact that several months had elapsed since the shares of Intotys worth over Rs 2 crores had arrived in Aunty-ji's depository account, he had not found it necessary to share the good news with her. Aunty-ji was still under the belief that she possessed only 100 shares of Intotys worth a mere Rs 1.2 Lakhs.

Hence, her happiness knew no bounds when Varun landed up at her house one evening with a cheque for Rs 5 lakhs, claiming that it represented profit made on trades carried out in her account during the preceding month. In reality, he was selling her own shares and returning a small portion of her capital back to her.

The old lady had no clue as to what was happening in her account, except that she was regularly buying and selling stocks as per the able recommendation of her relationship manager, in whose abilities she had complete faith. He was a godsent gift to her; so clever, yet so modest, claiming that it was sheer luck and God's will that were responsible for the exceptional returns in her account and not his trading skills. Varun diligently delivered Rs 5 lakh cheques every month, relishing the patties and pastries from Wengers that awaited him at every visit.

These luxuries had deadened the voice of his conscience.

"If it wasn't for me, Aunty-ji would never have had this windfall. The shares would have rotted away in some god forsaken corner of her house, and never seen the light of day. Since I am the lucky charm in her life, it is only fair that I gain some indirect benefit from her windfall. Not much, just a little to wet my beak every month."

He was confident that Aunty-ji wouldn't mind his indiscretion. Of course, there was no need to tell her. Actually, she was lucky that he was well meaning. Had he been like other relationship managers, he would have had the entire lot of shares transferred to his own name, leaving Aunty-ji old and poor.

On the personal front, things were not so good. He had become more independent and assertive. He no longer appreciated his father's meddling in his affairs. Arguments between them increased in frequency and ferocity. Finally, a month earlier, upset at his father's constant bickering, he had decided to move out of their house. He now lived in a small studio apartment, enjoying his new found freedom. He did miss them very much sometimes, but it was a small price to pay for his freedom.

"Don't you go all mushy now! Stand your ground. There is no going back. Otherwise the old man will never treat you with respect like an adult. It is important that they see me for who I really am."

However, his parents hadn't imagined life without him and were devastated by his decision.

Anil's professional life was a little topsy-turvy. From being the darling of his boss one month, he would be at the receiving end the very next. But this was by design. He could have relaxed and taken it easy at the cost of making less money, but this was not acceptable to him.

He put into play a unique action plan. He would pursue the revenue target in a given month only if he felt confident that he would qualify for the incentive. The first week of the month was extremely critical for him. If he performed well during this time and had a high probability of making the incentive, there was no stopping him. He would go on a rampage looting clients left, right and centre, doing whatever else was required to meet the target.

However, if he felt that the target was beyond his reach, then no matter how much pressure was put on him, he wouldn't do any revenue numbers; instead he utilised his time in opening new accounts and collecting fresh margin money, preparing for the next month.

Anil had figured out that they couldn't really fire a guy who hit the incentive benchmark every alternate month. He represented both the hope and the potential of consistent performance in the future.

Like Aunty-ji in Varun's life, Anil had also found his lucky charm. He was a gambler called Nikhil Seth. He had met him at a bar and seduced him with stories of the volatility in the markets, the opportunities they represented to make money and the adrenalin rush of gambling. The following day, Nikhil Seth arrived in the office to open an account and before the close of day he was trading heavily. While he didn't understand the different types of trading instruments, like all good gamblers he had a feel for the markets and understood human psychology better than others.

Compliance Strikes Back

Anil walked back into the office at noon from a client meeting and found everyone standing in the corridor. This wasn't normal. Relationship managers should have been busy pushing trades down the throat of unsuspecting clients. Something was wrong.

'What's the matter, buddy?' he asked Varun.

'Sunny has just returned from a meeting with compliance,' he replied. 'He has been going nuts ever since.'

'Why? What happened?'

'They have made some major changes.'

'Like what?'

'They came across multiple client accounts with the same email id.'

'So? What's wrong with that? Some clients are not internet savvy. My *milkwallah*s don't have an email account, but want to trade. What am I supposed to do?'

'I don't know, buddy. But from now onwards, the account opening department will call each and every client on their registered phone number to verify it and also confirm their email id. Only after that will the account be opened.'

'Oh shit! So now, not only do I have to create separate email ids for my *milkwallahs*, but also prepare the dumb fucks to answer these verification calls.'

'Yeah, looks like it,' said Devika. 'By the way, all these changes were recommended by your dear friend.'

'Who? Pooja? Are you serious?' exclaimed Anil raising his hands in despair.

'I had almost begun to miss my catfights with her,' said Devika. 'Now I know what she was up to all this time.'

'This isn't the only change. There are several others,' said Varun.

'Every order is taken by the dealer on a recorded line, right? However, in the past some clients disputed the orders stating that the voice on the recorded line was not theirs.'

'Oh shit! They caught this one too,' said Anil smiling.

'Why? What were you up-to?' asked Varun.

'Nothing dude, sometimes I would step outside for a smoke and call up the dealer, pretending to be the client.'

'But surely the dealer recognised your voice,' said Devika.

'Not my dealer, madam. Someone else's. We have this small group, wherein we place orders for each other.'

Varun and Devika looked at each other in bewilderment.

'WTF? You have been keeping busy, haven't you?' said Varun sarcastically. 'When were you planning to let us in on your little secret?'

'Don't be upset, buddy. Look at your faces. I knew you two wouldn't approve of it,' replied Anil. 'Anyway, what is the process now?'

'The dealer will call the client on his registered number and take the order.'

'What if the dealer is in your pocket and does exactly as you dictate?' asked Anil.

'Oh my god! Will you stoop so low now?' said Devika.

'I am just asking, guys,' replied Anil.

'You aren't merely asking, you are already considering it,' said Varun.

'Now you guys are being judgemental,' retorted Anil.

'My friend, without being judgemental, I advise you, don't even think about doing anything that's brewing in your mind. You will be caught red handed. Compliance will verify each and every trade at the end of the day by calling up the clients independently,' said Varun.

Anil didn't reply but looked visibly shaken.

Shahi Maut

A few days later, Varun accidently ran into Pooja. She was visiting his office for some administrative work and they came face to face with each other. It was an awkward moment for both of them. They exchanged pleasantries and then there was silence.

Trying to break the ice, he enquired about the changes implemented by compliance.

'Were they recommended by you?' he asked.

'Yes,' she replied.

'Business is drastically down. Anil is feeling the brunt of it.'

'Am I supposed to feel sympathetic?' she retorted.

'No. I didn't say that,' he replied.

'You guys are my friends. But this is work. And, when it comes to work, I don't make compromises.'

'Just that you were one of us, not so long back.'

So? Does that make a wrong, right? You guys never fail to amaze me. Such creativity gone waste,' she said sarcastically.

Varun was taken aback by her aggression. Here he was trying to make conversation and she was piling on to him.

'Excuse me,' he said. 'Not everything we do is wrong. We also face genuine problems.'

'Like what?' she asked.

'Anil's *milkwallahs* are not internet savvy. But the account opening form requires them to have an email ID.'

'Ha-Ha! So, Anil decided to help out by giving all of them the same email ID.'

'Yes. What's wrong with that? They want to trade.'

'*Pappu123@gizmo.com*, that's the email ID on 40 accounts tagged to Anil. You know how bad that looks,' she replied. 'These email IDs will not stand the scrutiny of the regulator for even a minute.'

'Yeah! You are right. I would have chosen a better name,' replied Varun.

'This is a joke for you, isn't it?' she said. 'How can you be so casual about everything? You are playing with people's lives.'

That was the end of the conversation. Varun wanted to clear the air and apologise, but she walked out on him.

After market closing, Varun met Anil and Devika.

'We have to find a solution,' he said. 'I wouldn't be surprised if these changes by compliance are only the beginning.'

'More changes? Are you serious? I won't even survive these for long,' said Anil.

'I think we need to re-evaluate our entire strategy,' said Devika. 'The problem isn't with our ability to get new clients or source fresh money from clients.'

'I second that,' said Varun. 'We have a leaky cauldron on our hands. We should try to plug the leak instead of running senselessly looking for new clients and money.'

'Plug the leak?' asked Anil. 'You mean not kill clients? How do we do that?'

'By not trading aggressively, I guess,' replied Devika.

'Thank you, darling! And who do you propose will do my numbers?' asked Anil sarcastically. 'I am not as lucky as you, when it comes to well-wishers.'

'There must be a solution,' said Varun.

'Give me a few days,' Devika said. 'I will find out how the others are dealing with this situation.'

On that note they left the bar. For the first time, Anil had not finished his beer.

Devika had a task at hand. She knew that the solution lay hidden somewhere in the work schedule of successful relationship managers. It was a good starting point. She hoped to decipher some trends or best practices. Were they successful because they had a large number of clients, or was it because they were skilled traders?

It wasn't difficult for her to get their attention. After meeting a few of them, she figured that the solution wasn't straightforward. It was complex and depended on a number of factors, each of which was difficult to replicate. However, there were a few trading ideas which could be easily executed to increase the revenue. She made a note of these before she met with the boys again.

'Did you find the answers?' asked a nervous Anil. 'My job depends on it.'

'Of course, I did,' replied Devika. 'But most of them are habit forming and based on inculcating best practices.'

'Who has the time for that!' replied Anil.

'Exactly my point,' she said. 'Hence, I concentrated on learning a few trading tricks that will give immediate results.'

'Now that's my girl,' said Varun. 'I knew we could count on you.'

'Come on, what are you waiting for?' said Anil. 'Shoot.'

'If we went to a shooting range for target practice, who do you think will win amongst us?' she asked.

'WTF! When I said 'shoot', I meant tell us your findings,' said an agitated Anil.

'Wait, I am coming to that. Don't lose patience yet, answer my question please.'

'It depends,' said Varun.

'On what?'

'How many bullets we have and how good our aim is.'

'Exactly! Similarly, our performance depends on the quantum of margin money and how efficient we are in generating revenue.'

'The first bit is obvious,' said Anil. 'But what do you mean by efficiency?'

'Efficiency in trading is the quantum of margin money you need to generate a given amount of brokerage income,' said Devika. 'If you generate a brokerage income of Rs 10,000 from Rs 1,00,000 margin money, then your efficiency is 10 per cent.'

'Generally speaking, efficiency improves over time as you become more skilled,' said Devika.

'I don't think so,' replied Anil. I am quite sure that my clients are dying faster than before.'

'You are unique, buddy,' said Varun laughing. 'These assumptions don't apply to you.'

'Last month my efficiency was 8 per cent. Is that any good?' he asked.

'There is room for improvement,' replied Devika. 'There are relationship managers with an efficiency of 15 per cent and then there are a few with an efficiency in excess of 20 per cent.'

'Enough of this bullshit,' said Anil. 'How can I improve my efficiency?'

'You can improve efficiency either by entering into profitable trades or by entering into 'efficient trades' i.e. trades that don't lose much money but earn good brokerage.'

'Varun, your ex mentor Tiwari-ji falls in the first category. He has a high percentage of profitable trades and therefore enjoys a very high level of efficiency. However, this skill takes years to master.'

'Yeah! I can vouch for that,' said Varun. 'I lost all my clients playing musical chairs with the market. Every time I thought they would move up, they fell down and vice versa.'

'That's why we should concentrate on efficient trades,' replied Devika. 'I met a relationship manager who is the king of efficient trading and has given many clients a *Shahi Maut*.'

'*Shahi Maut*!' said Anil. 'Sounds like one of those low budget horror movies. Madam, please don't speak in this cryptic language. Tell me something that I can understand.'

'If a client generates more than 25 per cent brokerage income on his margin money, it is called a '*Shahi Maut*' or an 'Honourable Death'. Instead of losing money to the markets, he dies for a noble cause, supporting us lesser mortals.'

Anil looked visibly relieved. For the first time he understood the drift of this conversation. They all had a hearty laugh.

'More on this tomorrow,' said Devika. 'Let's enjoy our drinks now.'

Later that night, when Varun returned to his house after a few drinks too many, he perused through the missed calls on his phone. He had not paid attention to his phone at the bar, being deeply engrossed in his conversation with Anil and Devika. He was surprised to find five missed calls from his mother. With a sense of dismay he remembered that it was his father's birthday. This had never happened before. He looked at the time. It was well past midnight, perhaps too late to call back.

"I must call and wish him first thing in the morning. How could I forget his birthday? He is going to really shout at me and say all kinds of sarcastic things, but I deserve it this time."

He didn't know it, but his father stayed awake all night waiting for the phone call that never came.

The next morning, Varun got busy swindling people and the call was never made.

Time to Revive the Milkmen

An efficient trade was meant to generate brokerage income while ensuring that there wasn't any significant loss in the account of the client. For a given level of brokerage income, the smaller the loss, the more efficient the trade.

Devika had learnt two types of efficient trades. Both the trades involved futures and options.

'Devika, how do you convince your clients to buy futures,' asked Varun?

'I tell them that it is the same as buying a stock. When the stock goes up, the future goes up. Except, the future has a limited life span.'

'Then why shouldn't they buy the stock instead?'

'Because, futures are cheaper. You can build the same position by investing only 15-20 per cent of the money. Clients never ask me questions thereafter.

'Good argument,' smiled Varun. 'You can proceed with your findings.'

'The first type is called a 'null' trade,' she said. 'You buy a future of the current month and simultaneously sell a future of the next month for the same stock or index.'

'But wouldn't they cancel out,' asked Anil.

'Nope, they won't. Because they are of different months,' she replied.

'Wow! In effect we have created two opposite trades,' said Anil.

'Yes, that's why the name, 'null' trade,' said Devika. 'It is a perfectly hedged position, each trade completely nullifies the impact of the other. The client will neither incur a loss nor a profit, and in the meantime we will earn brokerage on both legs of the transaction.'

'This is absolutely brilliant!' said Anil.

'No. It is not,' said Varun.

'Why?' asked Devika. 'What now?'

'First of all, this trade can only be done for a complete novice,' explained Varun in a calm voice. "Somebody who has absolutely no understanding of the markets.'

'That's just fine by me,' replied Anil. 'Almost 90 per cent of my clients don't understand the markets.'

'There is another bigger issue,' said Varun. 'In case we get caught, these trades cannot be defended.'

'You are being hypothetical,' replied Anil. 'Where is the question of getting caught when the client is a novice?'

'Exactly!' said Devika. 'You don't have to do this trade for every client.'

'No point arguing,' said Varun. 'Tell me about the other trade.'

'This is a binary trade, you either make money or lose it all,' said Devika. 'But it has one shortcoming, it can be carried out only once a month, on the last Thursday of the month.'

'Why only once a month? Why can't we do it more often?' asked Anil.

'Must have something to do with the expiry of futures and options,' replied Varun.

'Yup! It has,' said Devika. 'Half an hour before expiry, you buy out of money options i.e. options far away from the underlying market for your clients.'

'Isn't this what Pinto did?' asked Varun.

'Yes, it is. Except, Pinto didn't tell the client that the options would expire soon,' replied Devika.

'I am suggesting that you take the clients on board. Sell this as a high risk, high return trade. I am sure a lot of clients would like to take such a punt.'

'Hmmmm....This makes sense,' replied Varun.

'Double or triple your money within minutes, or lose it all,' said Anil. 'Some of my clients will be ecstatic with this trade.'

'Imagine how much brokerage you can generate,' said Devika. 'This trade is amongst the most efficient in generating brokerage. Sometimes, it can be as high as 30 per cent of the money invested.'

'Oh my God! This is the key to my problems,' said Anil. 'Time to revive the milkmen and the bus drivers.'

Have You Ever Seen a Horse Race?

Anil casually walked to the shop of Bittoo *chaiwala* with two sweets in his hand.

As soon as Bittoo, the proprietor of the small tea shop saw him coming, he started pulling down the shutters.

'Oh My God! He has come again.'

He had good reason to do so. Every time he had met Anil in the past, he had lost money. Despite this experience, he always ended up giving him more. The amount didn't matter, anything would do. Anil was such a storyteller, he would spin one story or another and take money from him. As a result, the poor tea seller had lost Rs 50,000 during the past four months, a small fortune for him. He represented a typical client in Anil's portfolio.

Anil looked at his watch—it was only 11.00 am.

'Uncle-ji, why are you closing the shop?' he asked. 'Is it a holiday today?'

'Bastard! If you have your way, I will be on a permanent holiday,' replied Bittoo sarcastically.

'Why Uncle-ji? Is business not doing well these days?' he asked without blinking an eyelid.

'You are a bad omen! You will not rest until my shop shuts down completely. I have promised my wife not to speak with you.'

'Have a positive attitude, Uncle-ji. If a shop has to close down, it will be that of your competitor. I am your well-wisher. I have even brought offerings from the temple.' Anil handed the sweets to him. 'One is for you and one for Aunty-ji. Please calm down and spit your anger. It is not good for your health.'

There was silence as Bittoo greedily ate the sweet.

'How are you, Chhotu,' asked Anil, gesturing at Bittoo's assistant. 'At least serve me a cup of tea.'

A few minutes later the ice had been broken and the shutters were up again. It was business as usual. Anil sat gossiping with Bittoo about everything under the sun, from the neighbour's wife and Uncle-ji's dog who always crapped on his front door, to Chotu's planned marriage. Everything, except the reason he was at the shop today.

As he was chatting away, Anil noticed one of Bittoo's clients sipping tea and sifting through the lottery page of the morning paper. Anil had found his opening. He immediately approached this person.

'Uncle-ji, have you ever bet on horses?' he asked loudly, knowing well that Bittoo *chaiwala* was listening.

'No,' replied the client, a little bewildered.

'Uncle-ji, then you have never experienced the thrill of gambling. Lotteries are so boring and mundane. You buy a ticket and wait for the result to come out the next morning. Where is the excitement and thrill in that? On the other hand, when the race commences, the excitement, the ear shattering noise of the crowds cheering for their horses is just mind boggling.'

'Really?' said the client looking excited. 'Where can I bet on horses?'

'At the Royal Polo Club,' replied Anil. 'But they won't let you enter unless you smoke a cigar and are driven in a big car by a chauffeur.'

The excitement died on the client's face.

'But don't worry, Uncle-ji. I might have the perfect product for you. It is not a horse race, but it offers the same thrill and excitement. And guess what? The odds are even better.'

Soon, Anil was in the midst of an animated discussion with the client, surrounded by a growing crowd of curious onlookers.

'Uncle-ji, this race happens only on the last Thursday of the month. However, instead of a racing track, it happens on the National Stock Exchange.'

'It is a winner takes all race, wherein you can double or triple your money within a matter of minutes. However, instead of betting on horses, you bet on something called options.'

'Options? What are those?' asked the client.

'Uncle-ji, they are similar to the horses that run on the race track. All you need to know is that if your option wins, i.e. the trade goes in your favour, you will make tons of money.'

He now had their undivided attention. Their eyes followed his every hand movement as if it were a proxy for the movement in the underlying market. By the time the discussion ended, he had three prospective new clients who wanted to ride horses in the stock market.

As he got up to leave the tea shop, there was a tap on his shoulder. It was Bittoo *chaiwala*, who had been listening keenly from behind the shop counter.

'Won't you take money from me?' he asked.

'No way! You will get me killed. I don't want to get into trouble with Aunty-ji.'

'Don't worry. This will be our little secret,' he said.

And Anil happily walked away with three phone numbers and a Rs 20,000 cheque in hand. The day had started on a good note and it was time to take the bus back to the office. Except, this wasn't any ordinary bus. The driver was his client and like all drivers, he enjoyed racing.

'Uncle-ji, have you ever seen a horse race?' he asked.

The Lord Only Helps Those Who Help Themselves

It was the last Thursday of the month, the day on which futures and options contracts for the current month expired, the day for which Anil and Varun had been waiting eagerly.

Both of them had greased the palms of the head of the risk department with a packet of cigarettes to ensure that they had unfettered access to trading during the last half hour before market closing.

Anil looked at his watch. It was 2.45 pm. In another 45 minutes, the options of the current month would expire. He was surrounded by half a dozen clients, including Bittoo *chaiwala,* who had come to the office to ride the horses that ran on the exchange.

'Bittoo sir, enjoy the tea and the cookies. They are on the house,' Anil said. 'We have 15 minutes before the race begins.'

At the other end of the room, Varun stretched himself and concentrated on the trading terminal in front of him. Nifty (index) futures were trading at the 8160 level, the 8200 strike price call option was trading at a premium (price) of Rs 5. If the market moved up in the last 45 minutes to beyond 8200 level, these call options of the 8200 strike price would come into money. However, if the market remained below the 8200 level, then these call options would continue to remain out of money and consequently their premium would fall to zero at market closing.

Varun had spent the better half of the previous fortnight identifying retail clients who would be interested in this trade. After going through his portfolio, he had zeroed in on those clients who had small sums of money ranging from a few thousand to ten thousand rupees in their account. This sum was too small to make any difference to their lives. However, if they undertook the options trade, not only would they enjoy the thrill and excitement of trading, but would also have a fool's chance of winning a big sum of money. He had approached 15 of them with this idea and after a little persuasion 13 had agreed. This list of 13 clients was with his dealer, who eagerly awaited further instructions.

Varun knew from experience that the markets would move only after 3.00 pm i.e. in the last half hour of trade. The Nifty future was moving in a small range of five points, 8155-8160. With every passing minute, the time value of the options declined and consequently the premium of the call option fell. At 2.58 pm the price of the 8200 strike call option had fallen to Rs 2.

He could hear Anil's voice in the background yelling at his clients to start buying. He decided to wait a little longer.

As the clock hit 3.00 pm, the market suddenly dived to 8150 and consequently the price of the call options fell to Rs 1.20.

'Let the game begin,' he yelled, gesturing to his dealer to commence making the calls.

The dealer started dialling one client after another on the list in front of him, buying 1000 or 2000 or whatever number of options the money in their account allowed them to buy, leaving 30 per cent behind to meet the brokerage cost and other exchange charges. In two minutes, they had bought 20000 options for their clients.

While the market was still consolidating at 8150 level, the price of the 8200 call option had risen to Rs 1.4 because of sustained buying.

'Call up Aunty-ji now,' yelled Varun.

Aunty-ji had been anxiously waiting by the phone for the last hour. Varun had informed her that he had devised an excellent trading strategy which would make her lots of money. She had no reason to disbelieve him. Varun's trading strategies had consistently made her money. For the past six months, she had regularly received a cheque for Rs 5,00,000 from his office.

Unknown to her, Varun had followed up with the registrar of shares and had been recently informed that a cheque for Rs 30,00,000 would soon hit Aunty-ji's bank account as pay out for unclaimed dividends. This would be the largest pay out Aunty-ji had ever received, thanks to his intervention.

Aunty-ji carefully read out from a piece of paper on which Varun had scribbled notes, repeating verbatim what she was supposed to say to the dealer.

'Son, please buy 200,000 call options of 8200 strike price at market price.'

The dealer punched the order at market price; it was a big order and consequently increased the price from Rs 1.4 to Rs 1.8 under its sheer weight.

Now, there was nothing left to do except to wait and watch the market for the remaining 26 minutes.

After meandering around the 8150 level, the market started moving up. With every passing minute, it gained momentum. First came 8160, then 8170 and 8180 followed in quick succession. People climbed on each other to get a piece of the action and the 8200 strike call option, which only eight minutes earlier had traded at Rs 1.20, now rose to Rs 5.

Anil was already yelling in the background asking his clients to square off their positions.

'Bittoo sir, don't get greedy. Taj Mahal wasn't built in a single day,' he said sarcastically. 'Please cut your position.'

But Bittoo *chaiwala* didn't listen. 'I will re-decorate my entire household today.'

Varun also did not lose his nerve and waited for a few minutes longer.

Then came 8190, 8195 followed a little later and just when it seemed that there was no stopping the market, that it would certainly cross the 8200 level, the market took a breather. Varun gave the sell instructions to the dealer. The 8200 strike call option was now trading at Rs 9 with 15 minutes still left for market closing.

The first person the dealer called was Aunty-ji. Her sell order caused the price to fall by a rupee. Then, the rest of the retail clients followed. Some sold at 8, some at 7 and 6 and then there were those who refused to sell, hoping to make big on their gamble.

Bittoo *chaiwala* was one of them. He didn't know the golden rule of gambling—leave the table while you are still winning. The market fell from 8199 all the way to 8170 over the next 10 minutes. As the bell rang indicating the closure of the markets, the 8200 strike call option expired at a price of zero. Once again, Bittoo *chaiwala* would return home empty handed. He wasn't worried about the money he had lost, but what would he tell his wife tonight?

Varun went down for a quick smoke. He looked up at the sky and spoke out aloud to himself: 'Oh lord! You are amazing. When I tried to make money for my clients, they lost. Today, my only intention was to make money for myself. But you had other plans.'

From behind him came Anil's voice, 'The Lord only helps those who help themselves.'

They both laughed loudly.

Birds of a Feather Flock Together

'Good morning, Boss,' said Varun, beaming as he walked into Sunny's room. His confident body language reflected his performance over the past few months.

'Take a seat,' Sunny said. 'I was perusing through the incentive numbers for the last quarter. You have done rather well for yourself.'

'Thank you, Boss!' he replied. 'God has been kind to me.'

'A bit too kind, it appears,' Sunny looked at him sternly. 'Who is this woman client?'

Varun felt the intensity of his gaze. It would have been enough to unnerve most people, but not him. He smiled and replied calmly, 'She is my aunty.'

'Why are so many people interested in your aunty?'

'Perhaps, because she is rich and they are jealous.'

'That might explain the reaction of people in sales; but what is the reason for your popularity in compliance?'

'I don't understand,' replied Varun, the smile disappearing from his face.

'Here,' said Sunny, tossing a report at him. 'Look at it.'

Suddenly the pitch of his voice rose.

'Bastard, you have done a turnover of 326 crores in that account last quarter. This woman is 70 years old, for God's sake.'

Varun calmly read the compliance report.

After a minute, he looked up and said, 'I haven't done anything wrong. This report doesn't show any wrongdoing. All it states is that there is an abnormally high turnover in that account.

'You can check the records, boss. Every transaction is recorded and has been done with the consent of the client.'

'I don't need to check the records to know that something is fishy here,' replied Sunny. 'I am afraid that a big blob of stinky shit will fall on my head in the future.'

Varun kept quiet.

'Smart ass, what if I were to land up at this aunt's house tomorrow? Do you think she would stand up for you?'

Varun laughed. 'Boss, please don't do that. The last person who visited her house uninvited had the door slammed in his face. I worry that your fear of shit falling on your head might actually come true.'

Their eyes met briefly, sizing each other up.

'There is no reason for you to worry. There is only one God in my aunt's life, and that is me. These are merely allegations. Tell them to stop conjecturing and give evidence of wrongdoing.'

'Are you suggesting that there is absolutely nothing wrong?' asked Sunny.

'Not at all. Everything we do here is wrong. All I am saying is that all transactions are compliant, the client is in my pocket and swears by me.'

Sunny mulled over his reply. This had confirmed what he had suspected all along. Varun was much like him. He was driven by money. He didn't lose sleep over morality and was even willing to look the other way, if required. Maybe, it was time for him to show his cards and bring Varun under his patronage.

'Don't worry. I will take this up with compliance,' he replied. 'But you owe me big time, boy.'

'Try me out, boss,' replied Varun. 'I won't let you down.'

'Are you sure you can handle it?' said Sunny. 'If word gets out, I will personally see to it that you are kicked out.'

'If there is money to be made, then I am interested,' replied Varun.

'Ok. In that case, I have a few special accounts that need managing. I will have them mapped out in your name.'

'What do I need to do?'

'Nothing. The revenue will appear under your name.'

'What kind of accounts are these?'

'The kind that will make you rich.'

Varun knew there weren't any free lunches and asked, 'Boss, what do I need to do for this generosity?'

'Pay back 75 per cent of the incentive you earn on these accounts. In cash, of course.'

'Sure,' he replied.

'Also, I am on the lookout for more like-minded people.'

'How many do you require?'

'Another two-three should suffice.'

'In that case, look no further. I can recommend two people to you.'

'Can they be trusted?'

'Of course. Even better, I shall manage all the modalities for you. As far as you are concerned, you will only be dealing with me.'

'Excellent,' said Sunny, visibly happy. 'You are rather resourceful.'

Varun recommended Anil and Devika. He met both of them later in the evening and told them about his conversation with Sunny.

'You both owe me big time,' he said. 'I could have had it all to myself, but decided to look out for you guys.'

'Thanks, buddy!' said Anil. 'So we need to pay back 85 per cent in cash?'

"Of course you do. There are no free lunches and without me you would be nowhere."

'Yup! That's what he said,' replied Varun smiling. 'We are now part of his inner circle.'

FALLING INTO AN ABYSS

(Almost Two Years Later...)

He is Retired

Anil had always wanted to retire early. An incident when he was very young had made a profound impact on him. When he was in standard 5 in school, his class was asked to write a paragraph on their father's occupation. They all did, except for one student. This student merely wrote in his notebook, 'He is retired.' The teacher didn't believe his story, and presuming that the student had taken the easy way out, punished him.

It was only later, when the poor lad's father landed up in school that he was let off. He had written the truth. His father had indeed retired a few years earlier, and now enjoyed a life of travel, music, and golf. Anil didn't know what he would do post retirement, but the thought of retiring before 35, intrigued him. It kept him hungry and running.

It was for this reason that despite the easy money, Anil was always on his toes, not letting a single opportunity pass, running after new clients and following up with old ones. The fact that Sunny was unpredictable also kept him wary. He was part of his coterie, but he maintained his distance. Sunny was known to regularly drop his cronies without much notice or reason. One misstep could land you in trouble.

Varun and Devika, on the other hand, were completely dependent on Sunny's whims and fancies. Varun strongly believed that joining Sunny's coterie was amongst the wisest decisions of his life. In fact, he often wondered why he hadn't done so earlier. Perhaps, it was because he was blinded by his youth and misguided self-esteem. Money was easy and in plenty. The 10 per cent extra that he was skimming from the payouts made to Sunny by Anil and Devika also didn't hurt.

So Varun was becoming lazy. His penchant for money had not declined, but it was easily available in plenty. He didn't want to work for it. Even his visits to his beloved Aunty-ji had reduced drastically. He lounged around in office most of the time, consuming large amounts of tea. At the end of the day, he strolled to the bar, most often with Devika, who was spending more time with him than ever before. They would drink themselves silly till late evening, laughing, hugging, caressing and at times kissing intimately. In case, they got carried away and their public display of affection got too much for the comfort of others at the bar, the action shifted to his house.

A few months ago, another batch of fresh graduates had joined, bringing fresh blood to the organisation. Like them a few years before, the newcomers had run senselessly trying to make a living. However, very soon most had been butchered, either resigning or being fired. Their clients had been reallocated amongst the old timers, making things even better for them.

While some might argue that life had become too easy for the old timers making them lazy, Varun wasn't complaining. Life was good and he was enjoying every bit of it. But he had started having many disagreements with Anil, resulting in heated arguments, especially when Anil tried to make him aware of his excessive dependence on Sunny.

The share price of Reddy Oil & Gas had risen exponentially creating a trajectory of its own. The stock had hit a new lifetime high of Rs 652 recently on the bourses. On his part, Reddy sahib had stuck to the script like a leech, showing consistent growth of 15 per cent in the top line every year. He had stopped diverting money from the company, thereby improving margins of the business. All this had a favourable effect on the market.

In the initial months, the analysts hounded Reddy regarding his earlier announcement of selling and leasing back the rig to improve his cash flow. It was this announcement that had triggered the rally in the stock. However, as the share price of Reddy Oil & Gas crossed Rs 450–the price at which the FCCB conversion was to happen–the question lost its relevance. All queries now hovered around the performance of the company.

An Opportunity Beckons

One day, Anil received a call from one of his HNI clients whom he held in high regard. The gentleman invited him for drinks to his house and to meet a friend of his. Anil gladly accepted. He never let an opportunity pass, especially when it involved free drinks. But he was intrigued. He had never met this client at his house before. He wondered what this was about. Who was this friend he wanted him to meet?

A few days later, Anil walked into the palatial house located in Lutyen's Delhi, a bouquet of flowers in hand. The damn bunch had cost Rs 500—money which would have been better spent on smokes and alcohol. But niceties required him to carry something, lest he was forbidden entry by the butler!

After exchanging pleasantries with his client at the patio, he was escorted to the living room.

'Anil, meet my friend Mr Punit Garg,' said his client.

Anil shook Mr Garg's hand firmly and then sat down next to the bar.

'Punit, Anil is a sharp chap. He has a business mind.'

Once the brief introductions were done, they moved on to the finer things in life.

'Anil, what would you like to drink?'

Anil stared at the bar, his eyes greedily examining one bottle after another. He always looked for the most expensive drink when someone else was paying. Aaah! There it was. He smiled. He had recovered the cost of his bouquet many times over.

'I would like to have a Yamazaki,' he said.

'Certainly.'

The evening had started on a good note. One drink led to another as they discussed the evolving political environment in the country. Anil's client did most of the talking, with the occasional concurrence from Mr Garg. Anil wondered what this meeting was about. Not that he was complaining. The whisky was better than the best he had ever had. But he couldn't quite put his finger on Mr Garg, who seemed to be a man of few words.

After a while, his host excused himself, leaving him alone with Mr Garg. Immediately, Garg took centre stage. There was nothing reserved about him now.

'I have a business proposition for you,' he said.

'You have my ears,' replied Anil, gulping down the whisky in his glass. The only thing Anil liked more than his whisky was an opportunity to make money.

Over the next hour, Mr Garg ran Anil through the intricacies of the business opportunity. He was extremely well informed about the happenings in Anil's office, including its underbelly.

As the magnitude of the opportunity dawned on him, Anil's pulse started racing. If executed appropriately, this opportunity was a game changer that would help him realise his dream of retiring early.

However, the key was execution. It was risky. Implementing it would have meant challenging the status quo. To see it through, one needed raw aggression and planning. This wasn't his cup of tea. It was more suited to Varun's style.

Finally Garg asked, 'Can it be done?'

'Of course!' replied Anil in his charismatic style. 'Give me a few days to figure it out.'

The next day, Anil tried to approach Varun several times but he could never catch him alone. Devika was always by his side. It was only after lunch that he was able to finally catch him smoking at the cigarette shop.

He immediately narrated the story exaggerating the payouts while underplaying the risks normally associated with the business opportunity. The first objective was to convince Varun to meet Garg. Once Varun was sold on the money, it would be a lot easier to get him to accept the risks involved in the execution of the plan.

After listening to him patiently for a few minutes, Varun agreed to meet Garg. Accordingly, a meeting was organised in the evening.

Anil was extremely happy with the way the meeting proceeded. Varun's body language was positive and he listened keenly to every word. They even exchanged visiting cards at the end of the meeting.

However, no sooner did they leave the premises than Varun turned to Anil.

'Are you crazy?' he said. 'How can you even consider bringing me to this meeting? This will upset everything for us.'

'I know it will,' retorted Anil. 'But look at the magnitude of the opportunity. It will change our lives forever.'

'It's too risky,' Varun replied. 'Don't you understand? If Sunny gets to know, we will be finished.'

'Where is that fire in your belly?' asked Anil.

'This has nothing to do with fire in the belly. This is suicidal. Sunny will get wind of this. He always does. Our industry is too small.'

Anil tried helplessly to convince him for a few more minutes, but Varun had made up his mind.

So Anil's dream of retiring before 35 remained just that, a dream.

The Markets are Frothy

Ever since it crossed the price of Rs 450, the stock of Reddy Oil & Gas had become increasingly difficult to manage. The institutions which had earlier blindly boarded the band wagon were getting off. Every time an institution exited, Salil-bhai was forced to become the counterparty, buying their shares and providing them with a smooth exit. He did so by taking ever increasing amounts of funding from brokers like Sunny.

When the time was right, he pushed up the stock further, attracting unsuspecting retail investors and distributed this additional holding to them. However, retail investors were jittery and emotional. There was a reason they were called the 'weaker hands'. They neither had the holding power nor the maturity of institutions, panicking at the first sign of weakness. Hence, as their numbers increased, the stock of Reddy Oil & Gas became unpredictable and volatile.

However, today Salil-bhai had bigger problems on his mind. As he analysed the '*Bhav Copies*' of the previous week, he was convinced that the overall trend in the market was changing. Week on week, the percentage of free float held by retail investors was increasing and that of institutions declining. Slowly, the stronger hands were giving way to the weaker hands. In stock market parlance, they were in the midst of the '*distribution*' phase. This trend was clearly visible across stocks manipulated by him. The writing was clear on the wall. The market was ripe for correction.

He quickly called up Kunal and ordered him to offload shares across counters.

'No more buying,' he said. 'We are only going to sell from now onwards. The market has moved up way too fast.'

'But why now?' asked Kunal. 'There is a lot of appetite in the market. It can go up further from here.'

'You always sell when there is exuberance and buy when there is none.'

'How much do you wish to offload?'

'Sell half of our positions across stocks.'

'Surely, not every stock?' said Kunal. 'Do you wish to sell even Reddy Oil & Gas? It was extremely difficult to manage it the last time we sold. You do remember, the FCCB conversion is due in a month.'

'I am aware of the risks,' he replied. 'But we have no choice. Once we lighten our positions, we will be better placed to handle any eventuality.'

'I am not sure if there is an appetite in the market to absorb such large quantities of shares,' said Kunal.

'Then create it, dammit.'

'Ok, boss!' Kunal replied. 'But it's going to cost money.'

'Give them five bucks for every share bought but not sold, and two bucks for shares bought and sold during the day. Also, issue a few trading calls in the market, both positive and negative. Pay some of those technical analysts if you have to. Also, the bulk sms providers. Tell Reddy to approach media houses via his PR company. We need everything on this one. We will have to generate a lot of volume to offload such large quantities of shares.'

Reddy is Going to Rock

It was a bright Wednesday morning, the sky was blue and the sun was shining in full splendour—a pleasant respite from the past few days which had been grey and cold. Grey, not because the sky was overcast, but because of the smog which had become an almost permanent fixture in the air.

Everyone was cheerful at the office, except for Anil, who sat morosely inside his cubicle in deep thought. In such deep thought that he had not taken a single sip of the tea that lay in front of him. Tea which had gone cold.

He should have been happy. His performance was good, he was at the top of the internal league tables, partly on the back of the special accounts handed over to him by Sunny. He had already achieved his monthly target with a few days to spare. This wasn't a bad situation to be in, then why was he depressed?

He had been in this state for a few days now. Every relationship manager had a godfather client, who accounted for most of his revenues. Varun had his old Aunty-ji and Devika her rich uncle. Nikhil Seth the gambler, as he was fondly called, occupied the same position in his life.

Unfortunately, Nikhil was not doing well lately. He was consistently losing money, even as he bet larger and larger amounts hoping to recover his past losses. Luck seemed to have deserted him. A few months earlier, Nikhil could do no wrong. Everything he touched turned to gold. But times had changed. And now he had begun drinking far more than before. What used to be victory celebrations earlier had now become drinking sessions to drown his sorrow. With every successive loss, he became more rowdy, loud and abusive. A few clients in the office had even complained about his behaviour. But Anil didn't give a shit about them.

However, what really worried Anil was that Nikhil had become unpredictable, often saying things that sent shivers down his spine. He was asking for ever increasing amounts of funding and other favours. Anil knew that he couldn't entertain these favours forever. It was only a matter of time before he had to refuse him. The situation was delicate and he wasn't sure how he should handle it. He wanted Nikhil to trade, as this was the only way he could recover his losses. He prayed that his client's good luck would return.

Yesterday, after many days of deliberation, he had asked Nikhil to take a break.

'You should take a holiday,' he had said. 'A few days of rest will revitalise you. The sun is inviting in Goa, the beaches are golden and women are aplenty.'

However, what he really wished for, was that the break would change Nikhil's fortunes. After some thought, Nikhil had agreed, much to his relief.

The fall in the revenue numbers was telling. The turnover that he used to achieve within the first hour of trade hadn't been done till noon. He stared distastefully at the cold tea on the table. Perhaps a stroll would lift his mood. He became aware of the buzz emanating from the trading room and decided to take a look.

He walked inside exchanging pleasantries with some of the retail clients who visited the office regularly. The market was up today. It had been the same for the past month. No one had predicted such a one sided movement. People who hadn't invested felt left out and were now scampering to buy stocks, driving the already overbought market higher. Then, there were the sceptics like Nikhil, who had short sold on every rise, and suffered huge losses in the process.

Going against the market was not for the faint hearted. It needed a lot of conviction and deep pockets. If you got it right, you could make a fortune. But if you weren't careful, you could lose it all. Anil felt happy. Thank God he had asked Nikhil to take a break. Otherwise, the poor lad would have lost today as well.

He was staring blankly at the terminals when he heard a voice call out his name.

It was the receptionist.

'What is it?' he asked.

'Sunny boss called up for you. Please call him ASAP.'

The bastard must have seen the trading volume and figured that something was amiss. He returned to his room and called up Sunny.

'What's up?' yelled Sunny. 'Are you guys taking a nap?'

Before Anil could reply, he added, 'That oil drilling company will see an upward circuit. I want to see your branch register the highest turnover.'

'Which oil drilling company?' he asked.

'Reddy Oil & Gas.'

'But Nikhil is on holiday,' said Anil.

'So? Call the son of a bitch. Probe the bastard. This might just be his lucky day.'

'How certain are you about the information?'

'Don't worry about the source. The movement has already begun. Catch it before it's too late.'

Anil put down the phone and relayed the message to the relationship managers in the branch.

He wondered whether he should call Nikhil.

He didn't trust Sunny. He was a first rate bastard who didn't give a shit about any client. He had made random calls in the past, just to prop up the turnover and revenue of the branch. But today he appeared to be confident.

He decided to wait and watch before calling up his client.

'Get me a cup of tea,' he yelled.

Then he sat back gazing at the trading terminal in front of him. A few minutes elapsed and nothing happened.

'Sunny, you are such a bastard,' he said drinking tea.

But just as he was thanking his stars for not calling Nikhil, there was a sudden spurt in volume and the stock jumped over 2 per cent in a matter of seconds.

'Holy shit! It's moving,' he yelled. 'The son of a bitch was right.'

He dialled Nikhil frantically, but didn't receive an answer. Shit, must be drunk. Anything was possible these days.

He dialled again. 'Come on! Pick up the damn phone,' he yelled.

The stock in the meantime was up 5 per cent.

'Holy shit! We are going to miss this one.'

He could hear the euphoria in the background. Clients were going ballistic in the trading room.

He dialled one more time. This time he was lucky.

'Anything urgent?' asked Nikhil.

'Of course, it is,' Anil replied. 'We must buy Reddy Oil & Gas. It will hit the upper circuit today.'

'What? I am in no mood to trade. You told me yesterday to take time off.'

'I know I did. But this is different. The stock is on fire. This could be the big one.'

There was some initial hesitation, but then Nikhil agreed. 'Anil, I am doing this trade because of your conviction.'

Anil's first feeling of excitement immediately vanished. He knew that he was in trouble. He had overstepped his brief and broken the golden rule of equity broking—the decision to trade is always that of the client.

But it was too late. There was no going back now.

'Open the limits and tell the dealer to call me immediately.'

Anil rushed to the trading room. He looked on as the dealer dialled the phone.

'Sir, you wish to buy 100,000 shares of Reddy Oil & Gas,' he said. 'I repeat. 100,000 shares.'

'Yes,' came the reply. Nikhil had just bought shares worth six times the money in his account. Anil gasped at the size of the trading position.

'Tell him to put a stop-loss,' he said, tapping briskly on the shoulder of the dealer.

The dealer narrated the advice to Nikhil. 'Sir, I would recommend you to put a stop-loss on such a large position.'

'No stop-loss,' replied Nikhil. 'It is for the weak.' They were all in, for better or for worse. Anil prayed it would be for the better.

By the time the trade was punched, the stock was already up 7 per cent. As soon as the order went through, it ran up another 2 per cent, by the sheer weight of the order.

Anil stood there anxiously biting his nails.

Within minutes, the stock was up 13 per cent.

'Call up Nikhil,' he told the dealer 'and square off the trade.'

The dealer did as he was told, but Nikhil refused.

'Boss, it's up 14 per cent now,' said Anil. 'We are making good money. Square it off.'

'Why are you jumping?' replied Nikhil. 'Today is my lucky day. I can feel it.'

'Boss, please listen to me, it's now 15 per cent up. Please square it off,' pleaded Anil.

'But didn't you say an upper circuit.'

'Yes, I did. But you never know these things. A bird in hand is better than two in the bush.'

Even as they talked, Anil heard cries of panic in the background. He quickly turned around to look at the terminal. The stock had suddenly dived 5 per cent in a matter of seconds. They were now barely breaking even on their position.

'Oh my God! Boss, the stock just crashed 5 per cent. We are still breaking even. We must square off our position immediately.'

'You bastard, what happened to the upper circuit?'

That was the last he heard from Nikhil who slammed the phone down on him. It seemed that Nikhil had raised his hands and left the matter to the divine.

The stock, meanwhile, spiralled downwards continuously.

By the time the divine intervened, it was already too late. The risk department squared off the positions at 3.00 pm. What could have been a good day had ended in a blood bath. Nikhil had just lost another fifty lakhs.

The stock closed at the lowest point of the day. It was a trap.

Anil was still mulling over his loss when he received a call from Sunny.

'How much money did you make? It went up 15 per cent after I gave you the call.'

He just lost it and went nuts on the phone.

'You said upper circuit. It was a trap. Nikhil Seth is finished.'

It took Sunny a few seconds to recover from the shock. No one had spoken to him like this before.

'You son of a bitch! I don't give a shit. I gave you a whore to fuck and you complain that her nails weren't manicured. I will fire your ass.'

In a matter of few hours, Anil had not only lost his most valuable client, but maybe his job. It was 6.30 in the evening. He was exhausted. He just wanted to go home, down a few whiskies and forget this day ever happened.

As he picked up his bag and switched off the lights to leave, he received a call from Nikhil.

He picked up the phone in a single ring.

'Are you alright? I was worried,' he said.

There was silence. After a few seconds, he heard the familiar voice, 'How much did we lose today?'

'The position was squared off at 3.00 pm. I kept calling, but you didn't answer. If we had squared the position earlier, we would have made a profit.'

'Don't give me stories. Answer my question. How much did we lose today?'

'Around 50 lakhs.'

There was a long pause. Anil could hear heavy breathing on the other side.

'What are you doing now?'

'I was just heading home,' he replied.

'Come over to the farm. We will drink tonight.'

'Sure. I will get the statements along with me.'

Anil knew that it was going to be a long night. Fifty lakhs was a large sum to lose in a day, even by Nikhil's standards.

Unknown to him, Sunny was sitting comfortably in a lounge bar, sipping champagne and counting the money he had received for his services.

Something is Wrong

Varun had seen Anil leave the office in a hurry the previous day. He hadn't thought much of it assuming that he must be heading to the bar. With a client like Nikhil Seth, beers were always on the house.

Varun often wondered what they spoke about every evening after market closing. There was some gossip in the office suggesting that their relationship was more than just friendship. But he knew otherwise. Anil had told him that Nikhil's magnanimity was no longer limited to alcohol, but extended far beyond to include entertainment as well.

Hence, when Anil didn't turn up at the office in the morning, Varun didn't think much of it. Must have had a few too many last night, he thought. The son of a bitch will land up at noon with a splitting headache, begging for coffee and aspirin.

However, when the clock ticked past 3.00 pm with no sign of his friend, Varun began to worry. As soon as the markets closed, he dialled his number. But the number was out of reach. Now he was really worried.

Had he crashed his bike after drinking the previous night? It wouldn't be the first time. He had seen Anil drive his bike under various stages of intoxication in the past. Once, he had fallen asleep while riding and had fallen into the roadside drain. Luckily for him, he had been quite slow and had managed to get away with a few stitches on his arm and torn jeans.

Varun tried to concentrate on his work, but his mind kept imagining all kinds of things that could have happened to Anil. It began to get dark. He still had a few emails to reply, but decided to come in early the next day to finish the remaining work. He was very, very worried and headed towards Anil's house.

He remembered that Devika would be waiting for him back home tonight. The thought of her wearing sexy lingerie, caressing him between his thighs sent his pulse racing. Only a short detour, he promised himself. There was probably nothing wrong. As he hurried outside, he received a call from Nikhil Seth. What the fuck did he want?

'Hello Nikhil,' he said. 'Anything urgent?'

'Come over to my farmhouse. Anil is also here.'

'Oh! Anil is with you?' he exclaimed, relieved. 'I have been trying to reach him since afternoon.'

'Yeah! He seems to have broken his phone again.'

'Nikhil, in that case, please excuse me tonight. I have some prior commitment.'

Nikhil's tone changed.

'I don't think you understand. I am not inviting you. I am ordering you to come. Cancel your engagement and come to the farm immediately.'

Nikhil had never spoken to him like this before, even when he was drunk. Varun cursed Anil for getting him into this situation. He'd much rather make love to Devika than listen to two drunkards. But he didn't have a choice.

'I am on my way,' he said.

He messaged Devika that he was caught up in office and going to be late. He did not want to deal with her questions just now.

She replied almost immediately, 'Ok, no problem. But if you are not here soon, the old man below your house will get the treat of his life.'

He cursed Anil again before starting his bike.

Nikhil's farm was almost an hour away. He had attended a few wild parties there during good times. He didn't remember attending any in the recent past.

By the time he reached the farm, it was pitch dark. He noticed Anil's bike standing in a corner. He parked his own next to it, turned on the torch in his phone and inspected Anil's bike. He was relieved to find that there weren't any fresh signs of a crash. Even if Anil had banged his bike, it was a minor accident. Or, it could very well be that he had merely fallen off it.

He went to the entrance of the farmhouse and rang the bell. Surprisingly, Nikhil opened the door himself, unsteady under the influence of alcohol.

'Good to see you, Nikhil,' he said.

There was no reply. Not even the customary handshake. Instead, Nikhil merely gestured to him to come inside.

"Something is not right. I should not have come. Should I just leave? I shouldn't have answered the phone. Why do I still try and be nice, I don't care about him. I just came because of Anil..."

He was still debating what to do when he heard the door being locked behind him. It was too late to act now.

Instead of proceeding towards the well-lit living room, they turned right towards the stairs that led to the basement.

Varun stopped, staring at Nikhil, 'We are going to the basement?' he asked.

'Yes, come along. I want to show you something.'

'Ok,' he replied, but he was now very uneasy.

It took Varun a few seconds to adjust his sight to the dingy basement. There was a single bulb flickering at one end of the room. The air was stale suggesting that the basement was sparsely used. There was this weird smell in the room, but he couldn't quite identify it. He slowly turned his head, his hands still holding on to the railing of the staircase and his eyes fell on the chair at the farthest corner of the room. It was occupied, but he could not tell who it was. The light from the bulb was not strong enough to kill the darkness.

He took a few steps forward. Then he froze.

Time to Make Amends

Varun could see the frail lifeless body of a person, hands and legs tied to the chair, head hanging down. He looked battered, as if every bone in his body was broken. He appeared to be the same weight and height as Anil, but Varun, his heart now hammering, hoped against hope that it wasn't him.

"I hope this is one bad dream. I want to wake up now. Someone throw water at my face. This is straight out of a movie."

He composed himself and turned round to stare at Nikhil, who was standing a few steps behind him.

Nikhil smiled, as if reading his mind. It was a creepy smile.

'Don't shit in your pants,' he said. 'I have nothing against you. Your friend is alive! He isn't worth anything to me dead.'

Varun rushed towards the chair; the weird smell became stronger as he came closer. It was the smell of bodily fluids, of blood, urine and human excreta.

He held Anil's battered face in his hands, trying to keep it all together. There was a big wound on the forehead, the nose was clearly broken, the left eye was swollen shut and the lips were cut. There was dry blood on his face, suggesting that the beating was from the night before.

As he examined Anil's face, his fear turned to anger. He wanted to yell, smash somebody's face. How could they do this to him? But he forced himself to think calmly.

"What should I do? How do I get out of this place? What the hell have they done to Anil? How can anyone do this? Even animals get better treatment."

His mind started racing. He looked around the room trying to figure out an escape route. Then he noticed the two bouncers standing behind him. He wasn't going anywhere.

He asked Nikhil, 'What do you want?'

'From you? Nothing.'

He took a deep breath of stale, stinking air. At least he was safe. Nikhil continued, 'They should be here any moment. I just want you to identify them for me.'

'Who?' he asked.

'His parents. You do know them, right?'

He knew them alright. He had celebrated Diwali parties at their house playing cards, but those were happier days. They were simple people contended with what they had. He dreaded seeing them under these circumstances, their only son battered, tied to the chair like a dog.

'Yes. I know them,' he replied. 'But don't you think we should call an ambulance, at least untie him. He is in a very bad shape.'

'You bastard, you only sympathise with your friend. The son of a bitch lost me 50 lakhs, trying to make his measly commission. You think I don't know what goes on in that slaughter house you call an office? You play with people's lives and their money without the scantiest regard for their well-being. You should be happy that he is still alive.'

Varun wanted to argue with him, but didn't. Partly, because he knew in his heart that Nikhil spoke the truth, but more importantly because he was scared for his own life.

'They will pay for his misdemeanours now. Someone has to make good my loss.'

Nikhil was still blabbering when with heavy, uneven footsteps, carrying the weight of old age and extreme stress, Anil's parents walked into the room. The expressions on their faces suggested that they were aware that something horrible had happened to their son. However, nothing could have prepared them for what they saw.

With a howl, Anil's mother ran towards her son, tears running down her cheeks, closely followed by his father. When they hugged him, Anil cried out in pain. As the realisation dawned on them that every bone in his body was broken, the crying became louder, almost hysterical.

'How you could do this to our son?' shouted Anil's mother. 'Look at him. He is so innocent, vulnerable, he wouldn't hurt a fly.'

They untied the rope that held him to the chair, only to watch his body fall to the ground. His muscles had given way and could no longer support the weight of his body.

Varun rushed to hold his friend, tears rolling down his cheeks. He picked him up in his arms like a child and carried him to the sofa in the corner of the room. Anil's parents were shocked and horrified. How could this happen to him? Varun had no answers. He covered his face with his hands and cried inconsolably.

'Now that the melodrama is over, let's get down to business,' yelled Nikhil Seth. 'Where are the property papers, Mr Shukla?'

Anil's father pulled out the papers from a polythene carry bag and handed them over to Nikhil, who handed them over to a bespectacled person standing by his side. He had probably walked in behind Anil's parents.

'Are the papers in order?' he asked.

The other person nodded his head in confirmation.

'Great,' said Nikhil. 'Please give me the promissory note.'

Nikhil walked towards the sofa, handed over the promissory note to Mr Shukla and said, 'Uncle, this document states that you owe me fifty lakhs and will make good this amount over the next year. In the interim, your house will remain as collateral with me. Should you fail to pay this amount, then I will be at liberty to take possession of your house and do as I deem fit to recover my loan. Please read the document once.'

Mr Shukla looked up, tears still rolling down his cheeks.

'Where do I need to sign?' he said.

'At least read the bloody thing,' said Nikhil.

'We just want to be done with this,' said Mr Shukla. 'Please tell me where I need to sign and then let us go.'

'Ok, Uncle. Suit yourself. Sign at the bottom of this page.'

The bespectacled man signed the document as the first witness and Varun was asked to sign as the second witness.

'This should do,' Nikhil said to Anil's parents. 'You are free to go. My driver will drop you back. Of course, I need not tell you not to go to the police.'

Then he looked at Varun.

'The same applies to you, smartass. Don't go yapping about this to anyone.'

Varun nodded. He just wanted to get out of this place. As he rushed outside, he saw the car leaving the premises. He decided to follow it to Anil's bachelor pad and ran towards his bike. However, by the time he reached his bike, he had an adrenalin rush. His body started shaking uncontrollably. He tried to kick start his bike but couldn't. His legs were shivering, no longer controlled by his mind. He tried again, but in vain. His head told him to leave this wretched place immediately, but he couldn't.

He sat on the ground and held his hands together, rubbing them vigorously, trying to get the blood flowing and stop the shivering. But it wouldn't work. After a few minutes an idea struck him. He got up slowly and walked towards Anil's bike. He searched for it diligently, that quarter bottle of whisky that Anil always carried. It was hidden on the right side of the pouch. He had never needed alcohol like he did tonight. He opened the bottle and drank it greedily in one go. It must have been at least half full. As the spirit went down his throat burning his insides, he felt the warmth return to his body. After a moment's rest, he kick started the bike and drove it like a maniac, deciding to visit Anil's house first thing in the morning.

By the time he reached home, it was midnight. The house was empty. He was glad that Devika had left. She would have asked him too many questions; questions that he couldn't have answered. She was obviously pissed with him, but he would deal with that later.

He lay in bed going over and over the happenings of the night, hoping that the whisky would put him to sleep. But it turned out to be the longest night of his life. For the first time, he felt an emptiness inside himself. He missed his parents. He missed his papa dearly.

Finally, at 5.00 am he couldn't take it anymore. He got up, took a quick shower and left for Anil's place. He found it locked. A closer look confirmed his worst fears. They had left in a hurry, perhaps never to return to the city again.

He drove to his parents' house and rang the bell. His father opened the door. No words were exchanged. He just gave the old man a tight hug, then walked into his room and lay down on the bed.

His father yelled from the living room, 'I still haven't forgiven you.'

He smiled. It was good to be back home. He closed his eyes and slept like a baby.

The Funeral Procession

Varun spent a few days at his parents' house, surrounded with love and affection. He switched off his phone and cut himself off from the world, hoping to heal his mind. But every time he closed his eyes, he saw a broken, lifeless body tied to the chair. Except, this body was not Anil's, it was his.

News about Anil spread through the office like wild fire. No one knew exactly what had happened, except that he had left in a hurry and they assumed it was because he had lost Nikhil Seth's money. No one blamed him, but none, not even Devika, felt any sympathy for him or any anger on his behalf.

'What the hell was he smoking to have done something so stupid,' she said, disgustedly.

It was business as usual in the office. Nothing had changed. It reminded Varun of the public apathy every time there was a train accident. It happened every year and almost always for the same reason—human error. While there was initial shock and horror, in a very short time the casualties became mere statistics in some report which no one bothered to read or implement.

This attitude reflected the broader degeneration in society. People are so busy making money that little else matters to them. Unless, of course it happens to someone they know or to them. Varun had also not cared a rat's ass when some other relationship manager got into trouble.

He felt differently this time only because it had happened to someone close to him, someone he knew well and cared about.

Relationship managers got into trouble with clients so regularly that it had become part and parcel of the job. Such incidents were soon reduced to mere gossip sessions between drunk colleagues, or preached as case studies to new recruits to teach them what not to do in the organisation.

It was 8.45 am when Varun reached the office gate. Something seemed amiss. The front gate was locked and there was a lot of private security deployed at the office. He pulled out his identification card and was let in and the gate was promptly locked behind him. This had never happened in the past. Which whorehouse ever locked its gates? They were always open for business, welcoming innocent, unsuspecting clients.

When he reached the reception, he saw relationship managers running around in panic. Such scenes were common in the trading room, but never outside. Even the receptionist, who otherwise greeted him with a big smile, looked worried. She was busy attending continuous phone calls.

As he took out his pen to sign the attendance register, his eyes caught a glimpse of the television screen behind the receptionist. Within seconds the enormity of the situation became apparent to him. There was only red colour on the screen, and red meant mayhem. The Dow Jones had crashed by over 5 per cent on Friday. Consequently, all Asian markets were deep in the red today and the SGX Nifty, which traded in Singapore and was a proxy for the Indian market, showed almost an 8 per cent cut.

Varun had switched off his phone over the weekend. The superficial sympathy of colleagues was tiresome. Instead he had decided to enjoy his father's one liners. What had seemed sarcastic and unbearable to him before, seemed very different when heard through the filter of love.

As a result, he had not heard of the crash in the market. Now, he didn't know what to expect. Of course he had not faced a rout in the market in his short career. Not that experience mattered on such days when most were rendered helpless, reduced to mere spectators. However, thanks to the incident of the prior week, he hardly had any significant trades in the market.

He remembered Tiwari-ji's horror stories. They all centred on the guys in risk. This was the kind of day when they went on a rampage and settled all their past scores. As Tiwari-ji aptly put it, 'A hundred blows of the goldsmith was equal to a single blow of the ironsmith.' They were easy to spot, the only ones with smiles on their faces.

He found Tiwari-ji sitting calmly in his chair drinking tea.

'Sit down,' said Tiwari-ji. 'Will you have a cuppa?'

'No,' he replied. 'How can you sit here drinking tea?'

'Why? Have they started charging for it?'

'No. I mean how can you be so calm today?'

'Didn't I teach you to cut your positions before leaving the office?' he replied. 'It was meant for a day like this.'

'So you don't have any outstanding positions which haven't been paid for?'

'Very few. Nothing to lose sleep over. And you?'

'Neither do I,' replied Varun. 'I haven't been active for the past few days.'

'I heard,' he replied. 'Let me know if you want to talk about it.'

'Thanks Tiwari-ji. I will,' he replied. 'What kind of market opening are you expecting?'

'They should hit downward circuit within seconds.'

'Downward circuit?'

'Yeah, the exchange has *circuit filters*. These have been created as a safety mechanism against volatility, specifically for days like today. The first circuit filter is at 10 per cent.'

'But the SGX Nifty is suggesting only an 8 per cent fall.'

'Let's see what happens. Everyone will be forced to sell when the market opens. This isn't going to stop at 8 per cent.'

'What happens after it hits the circuit filter?'

'Trading will be halted for 45 minutes. People will recollect their thoughts and cool their nerves. You and I will enjoy a smoke. You are carrying smokes, aren't you?'

'Of course, I am. And, what will happen thereafter?'

'The next circuit filter is at 15 per cent. If the market falls that much, then, depending on the time of the day, there will either be a halt or trading will be suspended for the rest of the day. In that case, you and I can go to the bar.'

'Ha-Ha! You make it sound so inconsequential. Do you really think it will fall that much?'

'I don't think so. But we will definitely hit the first circuit.'

'Then, why aren't you doing anything about it?'

'It will happen within seconds. Why worry, when you cannot act.'

They both sat together staring at the trading terminal and waiting for the market to open. The markets didn't disappoint. As suggested by the SGX Nifty, they opened with a gap, down 8 per cent over the previous close. But within seconds fell further, hitting the 10 per cent lower circuit.

Very few relationship managers were able to act. Their despair was visible on their faces. Most just sat there staring blankly at the screen in front of them, holding their heads in disbelief. The few who did manage to place a sell order were not sure if the order had been confirmed by the exchange and waited anxiously.

'Awesome, Tiwari-ji,' said Varun. 'Your understanding of the market is unparalleled.'

Tiwari-ji just smiled. 'Now, shall we go for a smoke?' he said.

'Sure! But let me just take this call,' replied Varun, pulling out the phone from his pocket.

'Wait! What are you doing? Is it a client?'

'Yes.'

'Are you nuts? Switch it off.'

Varun did as he was told. Bewildered, he asked, 'Why?'

'The client will beg you to hold his position. But you cannot provide any comfort today. Why create undue pain and frustration for yourself?'

The clients didn't know that relationship managers were helpless today. Cheques had no value and cash was king. The ledger needed to have a clear credit balance. Even then, no one was certain that the position wouldn't be chopped off by the risk department. The morons were on a high and could have done anything.

'Oh! So that's the reason that all the landline phones are ringing.'

'Yeah! And as you can see, no one is picking them up.'

'Now let's go to the terrace for a smoke,' said Tiwari-ji.

'Sure! By the way, why is the gate locked downstairs?' asked Varun.

'What do you think will happen after you don't take their calls? The poor souls will descend on the office to try and meet you in person.'

'How many are we expecting, that we need to have security and a locked door?'

'Hundreds. When they realise that their positions have been chopped, there will be frustration, anger and hysteria.'

As they returned to the trading room, they could hear the Finance Minister addressing the public on television. The Government was doing its best to calm the investors

'We are no banana republic. We have sound fundamentals,' the television blared.

'The same bloody script,' muttered Tiwari-ji. 'At least be original.'

In the background, phone calls were being made to the LIC, GIC and the treasuries of the large PSU banks to buy and support the market, thereby providing liquidity and improving market sentiment.

A few minutes after the speech ended, the markets opened again. The effect of the background work done by the Government machinery was clearly visible. The markets climbed a few hundred points supported by institutional buying. The relationship managers scrambled to cut their outstanding positions and lighten their portfolios.

'If you need to cut any client position, now is the time,' said Tiwari-ji. 'This rainbow will not last for long.'

Varun rushed back to his seat and pulled out his daily report. He was still perusing through it, trying to decide on the course of action, when there was a loud cry in the office: the trading terminals had crashed. You couldn't put a fresh order.

'WTF!'

There was anguish and frustration and the hysterical relationship managers abused the IT department which was responsible for the upkeep of the trading apparatus. This breakdown had come at the worst possible time. How could you explain to a client that not only had he lost money in the morning rout, but he couldn't create fresh positions because the office terminals were down?

Sunny was in a rage in the corridor outside.

'Jayant, I will have your head for dinner,' he yelled.

The IT department reported to operations. Hence, as the head of operations, Jayant was finally responsible for this mishap. Sunny's deep hatred and distrust for him was well known and now Sunny had got the opportunity to strike.

The terminals were restored within two minutes, much to the relief of the relationship managers. However, before Varun could act, a relationship manager rushed into the trading room shouting loudly, 'They have started the Bolt.'

It was now too late to act, as there was a risk of chopping off the position of the client twice, once at the relationship manager's end and once by the risk department.

Everyone had known that Bolt would be started soon. It wasn't a question of 'if', but 'when'. Risk departments across brokerages were waiting anxiously for some stability and liquidity to return to the market so that they could begin to chop off client positions. They were unable to act in the morning, since the markets had opened with a gap down hitting the 10 per cent circuit within seconds.

The 'Bolt' was a trading terminal connected directly to the servers of the exchange. It did not have any trading limit and was meant for *proprietary trades* of the brokerage. It allowed for manual upload of files containing aggregate client positions which could thereafter be literally thrown into the market. It was an efficient killing machine that worked like the much dreaded 50 calibre machine gun. You uploaded the magazine consisting of thousands of bullets and pressed the trigger. The machine gun kept firing till it ran out of bullets.

The risk department uploaded aggregate stock positions across clients on the Bolt. If 100 clients held a 1000 shares of ACACA bank each, it would reflect as one single entry of 100,000 shares of ACACA Bank on the Bolt. As soon as the enter key was pressed, the system would throw 100,000 shares for sale into the market at market rate. The order would be executed so long as even a single buyer of ACACA Bank stood in the market. The corresponding destruction in the price of the share was irrelevant.

Within a few minutes, the risk department had chopped off client positions totalling over Rs 400 crores.

The impact of this merciless chopping was felt almost immediately on the markets. In seconds they stopped climbing and then after a minute of consolidation started tumbling down. It felt almost as if the risk departments across all the organisations had coordinated their activity.

Again there was hue and cry in the trading room as the markets plunged rapidly. Within 15 minutes, they had fallen below the 10 per cent mark and were now trading at the lowest point in the day. The volatility was so extreme that most market participants were literally paralysed. Their hard earned money and livelihood was being decimated in front of their eyes.

By now, hundreds of people had gathered outside the office and the private security was having a difficult time managing them. If it weren't for the locked gates, this crowd would have certainly broken through and entered the office. There was extreme grief and hysteria among the retail investors who had lost years of their savings in the market fall. The scene wasn't very different from that witnessed at a funeral procession.

At one point, the fall in the market was so extreme that a breach in the 15 per cent circuit appeared inevitable, suspending the trading for the day. But sense seemed to have prevailed over the investment community and there was some ferocious buying at the lower levels, taking the markets above the 10 per cent mark. By the time the day ended, more than US$ 150 billion of investor wealth had been destroyed.

The stock of Reddy Oil & Gas ended the day down by 18 per cent.

The Fine Line Between Bravery and Stupidity

Varun and Tiwari-ji had been sitting in the bar for the past hour drinking beer. They hadn't spoken much to each other during this time, each lost in his own world. While Tiwari-ji mulled over the happenings of the day, Varun was still thinking about Anil.

As Tiwari-ji ordered the third glass of beer, he asked Varun, 'Are you alright?'

'I am fine,' replied Varun. 'Why do you ask?'

'You are quieter than usual.'

'So are you.'

'Yeah, that's right,' said Tiwari-ji, looking at Sunny who sat a little distance away at the bar surrounded by a few of his cronies.

'Jayant's days are numbered. The only guy who could stand up to Sunny will be gone soon.'

'He should,' said Varun. 'Terminals crashing on a day like today is totally unacceptable. He has handed his head on a platter to Sunny.'

'That's the intriguing bit,' replied Tiwari-ji. 'Everybody thinks that the terminals crashed because of a technical issue.'

'It wasn't IT?' asked Varun, a little perplexed. 'What was it then?'

'I can't say for sure. But the head of IT is a friend and he swears there was nothing wrong at his end.'

'How else could the terminal have crashed?'

'There is one other scenario, but I must warn you that I am speculating. We could have been shut down by the exchange.'

'Why would the exchange shut us down?'

'We might have fallen short on margin.'

Every broker maintains some deposit or margin with the exchange to meet its contractual abligation towards the counter party. On days of extreme volatility, this deposit often falls short due to loss on outstanding client positions. In such a scenario, the exchange asks the broker to fulfil the shortfall in deposit and in the interim, shuts down his account to ensure that no fresh trades can be created.

'But isn't the operations department responsible for maintaining deposit with the exchange?'

'The risk department is.'

'Yeah, and risk reports to Jayant. Hence, Jayant still needs to go.'

'Well, that's where it gets interesting. According to the risk department, there wasn't any margin shortfall at the exchange.'

'Then what happened?'

'I don't know, but it doesn't add up. There is something fishy going on at risk.'

'Why do you say that?'

'The terminals restarted a few minutes after risk started cutting client positions?'

'Couldn't it be a coincidence?'

'It could be, but unlikely on this occasion.'

'Tiwari-ji, don't test my patience. I don't like this information in bits and pieces. Please tell me the whole story.'

'After spending a few hours with IT, Jayant was convinced that the reason for the shutdown was not technical. So he called up the exchange. The exchange confirmed that it had shut us down.'

'Why were the risk guys lying?'

'I don't know. However, their records on exposure and margin didn't match those of the exchange.'

'Maybe they just made a simple mistake.'

'Maybe they did, but then why don't they admit it.'

'Unless it was deliberate,' said Varun, an eerie smile appearing on his face.

Tiwari-ji looked at him inquisitively.

'I think I know what the hell is going on,' said Varun, now excited. 'The sons of bitches are under-reporting some accounts. This is the reason we were shut down.'

'That's a possibility.'

'They have been running a clandestine operation all this time. The fall in the market took them by surprise. They fucked up and are now pointing fingers elsewhere to cover their asses. I also have a fair idea which accounts these might be.'

Tiwari-ji silently mulled over Varun's words.

'We can't allow Jayant to take a fall for this,' said Varun, agitatedly.

'Cool down,' said Tiwari-ji. 'Why should we get involved in this nonsense? Let the two Titans fight it out.'

'Because, we don't have the luxury of time. Jayant might be out before he figures out what transpired.'

'I absolutely don't want to be drawn into any kind of controversy now,' replied Tiwari-ji.

'It was Anil last week and now Jayant. Someone needs to stand up to Sunny,' said Varun, heatedly.

'I have lived rather well by not being controversial.'

'Did you just say, you have lived well?' said Varun. 'You haven't lived, you have merely survived, by hiding and running away from responsibility your entire life. Please stand up for once, Tiwari-ji'.

I need to think this over,' said a visibly upset Tiwari-ji, shaken by Varun's barrage.

'Suit yourself,' replied Varun curtly. 'But I can't take this anymore.'

Varun suddenly stood up from his chair and charged towards Sunny. Tiwari-ji was taken by surprise. He tried to stop him but couldn't act fast enough. But he yelled behind him, 'You are drunk, don't do anything stupid.'

But that is exactly what Varun planned to do. He was simmering with anger and frustration. In his mind, Sunny was responsible for pushing Anil to the extreme. Otherwise, Anil would still be around cracking jokes today.

Varun wanted to punch Sunny in the face and knock the daylights out of him. But with the beer buzzing in his head, all he could manage was a slow jab that landed on Sunny's right shoulder.

The jab did little more than bruise Sunny's ego. But even that was an accomplishment as no one had ever challenged him before. For a few seconds, he didn't react, confused and shocked at what had just happened.

Meanwhile, his cronies held on to Varun firmly and waited for instructions from their boss.

'You son of a bitch,' roared Sunny, trembling with anger. 'How dare you?'

The commotion brought Tiwari-ji to his feet and he rushed to intervene. However, by the time he reached, Sunny had already landed a tight slap across Varun's face. The beer did help to absorb some of the impact, but Varun still shrieked in pain.

'Let him go,' yelled Tiwari-ji. 'He is drunk and does not know what he is doing.'

'Not so fast,' yelled Sunny, landing a punch into Varun's stomach. Varun puked all his dinner on the guys holding him, coughing and crying in pain. He couldn't breathe for a few seconds and fell to the ground.

'Keep your puppy on a leash,' said Sunny, as he walked out of the bar.

Varun groaned in pain. He wanted to shout, but there was no air in his lungs. All he could manage was a whisper.

'Sunny, how could you do this to Anil?'

But Sunny and his cronies were long gone. Varun's voice was too weak to reach anyone other than Tiwari-ji who bent over him, trying to help him up.

AWAKENING

A Relationship of Mutual Convenience

Varun left the bar and went home to nurse his wounds. The buzz from the beer was long gone and all that was left behind was pain. There was also the realisation that he had just committed hara-kiri.

He called up Devika hoping to get some sympathy. He didn't say much except that she should meet him at his apartment. Perhaps, he had an inkling of what lay in store for him.

Half an hour later, they were sitting together in his living room, drinking whisky. As he narrated what had happened, there was a look of disbelief on Devika's face. Soon, her voice became loud and desperate. The whisky was too damn weak to calm her nerves as she yelled and abused him at the top of her voice. There was not an iota of sympathy in her voice.

'You are such a dickhead,' she said. 'Why couldn't you just enjoy the good times?'

'But he was wrong!'

'Wrong? Are you serious? All we have ever done is wrong. But we kept our mouths shut and enjoyed the spoils. What the fuck got into you tonight?'

'But he is responsible for what happened to Anil.'

'In our line of work, it could have happened to anyone. Better Anil than you or me. Anil should have known better than to screw Nikhil.'

'How can you talk like this about Anil?'

'You are being emotional when you should be practical. Go back to Sunny now and apologise. Tell him that Tiwari flamed your anger. It is still not too late.'

'But Tiwari-ji had nothing to do with it.'

'It doesn't matter. Someone needs to be sacrificed for your idiocy tonight. You know that Sunny doesn't like Tiwari. Burn the son of a bitch.'

Varun kept quiet.

'Do as I say. In a few days, Anil's clients will be transferred to us, and we will be laughing all the way to the bank.'

'No, I will certainly not.' said Varun. 'I have done nothing wrong.'

'Fool,' said Devika, gulping down her whisky. 'You are a fool. Then go, be by yourself. I don't want any part in the shit you have landed yourself in.'

She rushed out without looking back. Varun knew that she was gone, perhaps forever. Their relationship was built on mutual convenience and it was no longer convenient to be associated with him.

He sat in his room looking at the glass of whisky in his hand, replaying the sequence of events in his mind as they had occurred in the evening.

"Would I have acted the same way had I not been drunk? Is Tiwari-ji trying to play me against Sunny? More importantly, with Anil and Devika gone, who can I turn to? Tiwari-ji? Perhaps not. He has never taken sides, nor is he likely to."

There was only one person he could think of at this moment.

"Will she entertain me, after what I have put her through? I haven't even been in touch with her for over two years. Devika wouldn't have it any other way."

But discreetly he had often enquired from Anil about her well-being. They ran into each other on a few occasions, exchanging pleasantries, the occasional eye contact, but nothing more.

"There is no harm in trying. She is my only hope."

He dialled her last known number hoping it was still in use. The bell rang a few times but there was no answer.

Moving to Greener Pastures

'Where is that thankless bastard?' asked Sunny. 'Has he come to the office?'

'I doubt it, boss.' replied Devika. 'He doesn't have the balls to confront you. Must be in hiding somewhere.'

'If I catch him, I will roast him alive. He had a few too many last night and hence I let him go. I was expecting to find him in my office this morning, begging for forgiveness.'

'Boss, I told him to do that. But he was adamant.'

'What's gotten into him lately?'

'I think it is Tiwari-ji. He has been adding fuel to fire.'

'Atul Tiwari? Can't be. He is a pussy. Anyway, doesn't matter. I will deal with both of them later. But for now I must reward you. You did the right thing by coming here.'

Sunny picked up the phone and dialled the back office.

'I am sending you an email. Kindly transfer all the accounts mentioned there immediately to Devika.'

'I guess Varun doesn't appreciate my generosity anymore,' he said. 'It's time he fended for himself.'

With a single phone call, Sunny had changed her fortunes forever. There was a hint of guilt in her mind, but she didn't let it show. There was no place for such emotions. She had done her bit and tried to drill sense into Varun, giggling with joy. She was moving on to greener pastures.

'Thank you, boss,' she replied with a flirtatious smile.

'Don't bother. We always take care of our own,' said Sunny, with a let's-get-to-know-each-other-better smile on his face.

What About Me?

His eyes were shut. He had a smirk on his face. He was perhaps dreaming, oblivious to the happenings in the real world. In one hand, he held an empty bottle of whisky, while the other lay inside his trousers.

He heard some random noise in the background, not loud enough to warrant action. Then the noise became louder. It was only a minute later that he realised the source of the disturbance was his mobile phone vibrating. However, by the time he opened his eyes it went silent. He wondered, if he should go back to sleep. There was very little to look forward to anyway. But something told him to glance at his phone. As he tried to focus his groggy eyes, he saw the empty bottle of whisky and smiled. Then he burst out laughing, pulling out his other hand from inside his trousers. With Devika gone, survival instincts had taken over. He was back to the good old days.

There were ten missed calls on his phone. Obviously, word about his misadventure with Sunny the previous evening had gone round the office like wild fire.

'They don't give a shit about my well-being, all they want is a piece of the gossip,' he mumbled. 'I don't even know if I have my job anymore.'

He deleted the first few calls from the call record. Then he stopped. Pooja had returned his call. Not once, but thrice. His heart leapt up. There was still hope. For a moment, he forgot about the beating he had endured the previous evening until the excruciating pain in his rib cage reminded him that all was not well. He limped towards the bathroom to wash his face. The faint imprint of Sunny's hands on his left cheek was still visible.

Thank God, he had a stubble. Otherwise, he would be a walking advertisement of his misadventure with Sunny.

He returned to his bed and dialled Pooja, his heart beating fast in anticipation. After a few rings, he heard her high-strung stressed voice.

'Varun, where are you? I am going crazy trying to reach you. I tried your phone several time over the weekend, but it was switched off.

"At least someone still cares about me. Maybe I misread the signals in the past."

'Any news of Anil? His phone still says out of reach.'

"Anil? She wants to know about Anil? What about me?"

'He has returned to his village,' he mumbled.

'Oh my God! Then all those rumours floating around the office are true?'

'Yes, unfortunately they are. He was beaten badly by one of his clients.'

'Why? What happened?'

Varun was now losing patience.

"All she wants to know about is Anil."

'Listen Pooja, it's a long story. All I know is that Sunny was behind it. I took him on yesterday and might be in a lot of trouble myself.'

'Oh! So that's why you punched him. I thought it was perhaps just a drunken brawl.

"She knew about it and still not a word of concern."

'Are you alright?'

"Finally."

'I am fine, Pooja. Thanks for asking.'

'By the way, I saw your girlfriend with Sunny in the morning. She was singing like a canary. I presume that those weren't words of praise, coming out of her.'

'If it's any comfort to you, Devika was never my girlfriend,' he said.

'I don't care,' she replied.

'I am not even sure if she is a friend anymore. She walked out on me last night.'

The line went silent for a few seconds.

'I am sorry to hear that,' she said.

"Ah! Finally some sympathy."

'There is no need to be sorry. I have not been very wise in my choice of friends, but I intend to make it right now,' he replied. 'In fact, I am not surprised that she met Sunny,' he said. 'We had a relationship of convenience. It had to end someday.'

Changing the topic she said, 'I met Tiwari-ji in the morning. He narrated the entire incident to me. You don't have much time.'

'I am aware. The only reason, I might still have a job is because Sunny has more important things on his mind.'

'Like what?'

'Jayant. He wants him out.'

'Looks like he will get what he wants. Jayant is under much pressure. He called me last night to carry out an investigation.'

'About the crashing of the terminals, I presume.'

'Yes,' she replied. 'How do you know?'

'An intelligent guess. Guess what? You are in luck. I am privy to some information that might help you piece this jigsaw together.'

'Oh! In that case, we should meet immediately. How fast can you get ready?'

'Maybe an hour.'

'Great! United Coffee House, lunch at 12.30.'

'Sounds good. Please find a table inside. I don't want to run into anyone from office.'

Don't Lose Your Nerve

'Boss, this is Ravinder, from risk.'

'What is it, Ravinder?' asked Sunny.

'Boss, there is an outstanding position of 50 crores in those accounts, which hasn't been paid for.'

'So? You have enough stocks as collateral.'

'In addition, we have an MTM (Marked To Market) loss of 10 crores on other positions in those accounts. I cannot hide such large debits. This needs to be funded.'

'Bastard! I am bending backwards to get Jayant fired so that you can take over his position and here you are whimpering like a bitch in heat.'

There was a moment of silence.

'Boss, you don't understand. There was absolutely no technical issue yesterday. The exchange shut us down because of a margin shortfall.'

'What the fuck? How could you let this happen?'

'The market hit downward circuit within seconds. We just couldn't act. As soon as the market opened again, the exchange shut us down.

I immediately gave the order to chop positions. Within minutes, we had chopped positions worth a few hundred crores and the terminal was back up again.'

'But I thought there was always a buffer margin? We always took care to ensure that terminals never crashed.'

'We did, but yesterday was not a normal day. How can one prepare for such volatility? I am worried that Jayant will find out sooner or later.'

'In that case, I better keep the heat on him and get his ass fired. Who else is aware about this fiasco?'

'Only I, boss. The exchange called up Jayant, but luckily, he wasn't in his room. The call was transferred to me. As soon as I received the call, I gave the order to commence chopping of positions.'

'Ok, let me see what I can do. But don't you fucking lose your nerve. It is only a matter of a few days. Hang on. Jayant is on his way out and you will be the new king of operations.'

Sunny wondered why the promoters of the company were taking so long to act on the matter. Jayant should have been sent packing by now. All he had done all these years was to create hindrances in the functioning of the sales department.

Respect Yourself, or None Will

Varun reached Connaught Place and walked into United Coffee House at 12.30 pm. He was glad to find Pooja occupying a corner table. As expected, she was there well before time.

As he walked towards the table, their eyes met briefly. She got up from her seat. He wanted to give her a hug, but seeing her hesitation, shook her hand instead.

'I have taken the liberty to order your favourite food,' she said. 'I hope your taste buds haven't changed.'

'Keema samosa and Nargis ke kofte?'

'Yes, and a butter naan to go with it.'

'Thanks. I wouldn't change that even if I was on my death bed.'

'You don't look very good.'

'I am starving. Otherwise, I am fine. But tell me about yourself? How have you been? What's going on in your life?'

'Not much,' she replied. 'Let's remain focused on the work at hand.'

But Varun didn't take the hint.

'A glowing face, manicured hands and a stylish haircut. What's going on lady?'

'I have learnt well from my past,' she replied. 'If you don't respect yourself, no one else will.'

Ouch! That was a curt reply. Varun wondered what to say and was glad that they were interrupted by the arrival of food.

For the next five minutes, there was near silence as he ate, hoping to ease the air. After finishing half of the naan, he looked up only to find her looking at him firmly.

'This is embarrassing,' he said. I am eating like a homeless man on the street.'

'Never mind,' she replied.

But he could see that she was getting annoyed.

'Why don't you tell me what you have found out till now?' he said.

'Finish your food, and I will.'

'Hey, I am getting conscious. Let's discuss as I eat.'

'Ok, if you insist.'

'The terminals didn't shut down due to a technical glitch.'

'I know,' he replied. 'The exchange suddenly shut us down due to margin shortfall.'

'How the hell do you know that? It is supposed to be all hush hush.'

'You should know better. Nothing remains hush hush in this organisation, even the walls have ears.'

'I guess you are right.'

'The question that needs answering is, why is the risk department adamantly refusing to accept that the exchange shut us down due to margin shortage.'

'Probably, because Ravinder doesn't want to lose his job. With Sunny going on the warpath for Jayant's head for this mishap, Ravinder's behaviour is understandable.'

'That could be a plausible explanation. But my convoluted mind tells me that there is more to the story than meets the eye.'

'Perhaps, you are applying yourself more than you should Varun,' she said sarcastically.

'And, what if I am right?' he said, a little annoyed.

She didn't reply.

'Tell me, Pooja, who gave the order to chop the client positions yesterday? Was it Jayant?'

'No, it wasn't. Ravinder took the decision on his own.'

'Doesn't that strike you as being odd? I mean the authority rests with Jayant.'

'Not at all. On the contrary, if he hadn't, the terminals would have remained shut for a longer period of time. Jayant, like everyone else, thought that there was a technical fault.'

'So you don't think Ravinder did anything wrong?'

'As of now, I don't.'

'What about the discrepancy, then?'

'Which discrepancy?'

'The one between our records and those of the exchange.'

'You know about that, too? Really, nothing remains a secret here.'

'Go on, explain to me the discrepancy in data?'

'Maybe, it was a mistake?' she replied.

'A mistake! How can you be so naïve?'

'Tell me you have more,' said Pooja. 'Otherwise, we are wasting time here. You are seeing intent, whereas these could be simply unrelated acts.'

'Ok, if that's the way you want it, then listen to my story carefully with an open mind.'

Varun told her about his meeting with Sunny over two years earlier, when Sunny had showed his cards for the first time. There were a few large client relationships which were managed by him directly. These relationships were so large, that their activity would have been noticed by compliance. In order to keep them under the radar, they were split into several accounts, and handed over to his confidants to manage.

'I was one of his confidantes,' he said.

Pooja looked up in surprise. 'Why are you telling me this?'

'Because I trust you.'

'You didn't keep in touch for two years, and now you trust me,' she replied.

'Listen, I made some mistakes in the past and now I have to bear the consequences.'

'Sure you do. But it's suicidal to take on Sunny. You had it going well. Why are you doing this?'

'Don't sound like Devika. Money isn't everything.'

'It was for you, till a few days back. What changed?'

'Anil happened. In my mind, Sunny is responsible for it. If we don't intervene, it will be Jayant tomorrow. Day after, it could be any one of us. Someone needs to stand up to him. What he did was wrong, and he needs to take the fall for it.'

'But why does it need to be you?'

'Now, you sound like Tiwari-ji. I don't have an answer why it needs to be me. All I know is that it is the right thing to do. The Pooja I used to know stood for what was right. Has time changed you?'

For the first time Pooja smiled.

'I was just testing your resolve. I wanted to be sure that you knew what you were getting into. Don't worry, if you want to clean this organisation, then I am fully behind you.'

'Thanks. This means a lot to me. Coming back to our discussion, such a large clandestine operation cannot be carried out without the active involvement of the risk department.'

'I agree with you,' said Pooja. 'Someone certainly knows about these accounts in risk. After all, they are the ones who give exposure, monitor positions and chop them in case they become dangerous.'

'Exactly my point. On the day the market crashed, both the reports i.e. Client exposure and MTM loss were wrong. It is my belief that these special client accounts were not included in either of these reports. This is why there was a discrepancy in the records of the exchange and ours.'

'As per my understanding, you always maintain an additional margin with the exchange to ride over market volatility. Was there such a buffer in margin yesterday?'

'Yes. We had a buffer. But it was an extremely volatile day.'

'You are right. It was extremely volatile yesterday. But you cannot rule out my hypothesis that the shutdown happened due to the additional exposure and marked to market loss on these hidden accounts.'

'No. I cannot.'

'Also, Ravinder is no hero. When the terminals shutdown, he shat in his pants. Cutting client positions was an afterthought to cover his track and save his ass. With Jayant on his way out, Ravinder will be anointed as the head of operations soon and all this will be shoved under the carpet, never to be found again.'

'No, he will not,' replied Pooja. 'Not if I can help it.'

'Now that's the Pooja I know,' said Varun smiling.

Varun pulled out a sheet of paper from his pocket and handed it to her.

'This paper contains the list of 12 special accounts. Run it through your back office system and let me know what you find out.'

'I will,' she replied. 'Keep a low profile till then. I will try to call you tonight. Once you have confirmed that my hunch is correct, we will need to move fast.'

'Yes. Very fast.'

Don't Put Me in a Spot

As soon as Sunny got off the phone with Ravinder, he dialled Kunal, Salil-bhai's assistant. Ravinder was right, it was essential to get the outstanding positions funded. Then, even if Jayant got wind of their clandestine operation, he wouldn't have anything to act on. Once, he had covered his tracks, he would go after Jayant with renewed ferocity.

Kunal was responsible for all day-to-day operational matters. Sunny had spoken to Salil-bhai only once, at the start of their relationship. Thereafter, all his interactions had been with Kunal. As if to emphasise the seriousness of the circumstances, he didn't exchange any pleasantries with Kunal and got straight to the point.

'There is an outstanding position of over 50 crores in the accounts.'

'I am aware,' replied Kunal, calmly. 'Where is the problem? This position has been outstanding for over a month.'

'Times have changed. It's not the same anymore. Didn't you see the volatility in the market yesterday?'

'But you have over 100 crores of stock kept as collateral. What are you worried about?'

'Reddy Oil & Gas crashed 18 per cent yesterday. I can't keep shares of Reddy Oil & Gas as collateral. It is too volatile. My risk department is losing sleep. You will have to close these outstanding positions.'

There was no response from Kunal.

'We also incurred an MTM loss of 10 crores. This needs to be funded immediately.'

The voice changed on the phone line.

'What Sunny, market takes a tumble one day and you start shitting in your pants,' said Salil-bhai. 'You are making me look very bad in front of Kunal. It was my decision to give you this business.'

Sunny lost his aggression immediately. He was no longer demanding, but pleading.

'Salil-bhai, it is not like that. I am currently under tremendous pressure from operations.'

'I am not doubting that, but where is your mettle? You are supposed to handle such matters.'

Then lowering his tone, he said, 'Don't get me wrong, I am not denying that the accounts will be funded. But this will take time. How am I supposed to organise 10 crores at just a minute's notice?'

'Ok. So by when can I expect the funds?'

'It will take a few days.'

'Can I send somebody day after tomorrow?'

'No, you cannot. Don't put me in a spot. My guy will visit you in the evening with Rs 15 lakhs for your troubles.'

'But Salil-bhai...' The phone was disconnected.

My Bed Misses You the Most

Varun was anxiously pacing in his living room for the past hour, waiting for that all important phone call from Pooja, the call that would decide his fate in the organisation.

It was well past 9.30 pm and he was hungry. The bottle of whisky on the dining table looked more tempting with every passing minute. However, he controlled his urge; he had to remain sober tonight. At least, till he discovered the outcome of Pooja's enquiry. If his hunch was validated, he would celebrate in style the whole night. If it wasn't, then he would drink silly to get over the mess he had created.

She should have called him by now. He wondered why she was taking so much time. He hoped that everything was going as per plan and she wasn't in any trouble. An empty mind was a devil's playground and all kinds of thoughts clouded his brain.

Finally, his phone rang. He glanced at the number before answering it. It was Devika.

"What the fuck does she want?"

He let the phone ring a few times, getting his thoughts in order.

'Devika, my darling,' he said, in a slurred voice. Where are you?

'You are drunk, as expected. I am not coming back to you.'

"I know that."

'I miss you, darling. My bottle of whisky misses you more. My bed misses you the most,' he said.

'Loser, I am not coming back. I told you to go and apologise to Sunny, but you didn't relent. What was I supposed to do? You didn't leave me any choice. I made peace with Sunny and sold both of you out.'

'Both? Who?'

'You and that Tiwari fellow.'

'Bitch,' he yelled. 'Is Sunny already inside your pants?'

'That's none of your business. Guess what, Sunny transferred all the special accounts to me.'

"Of course he did."

'Where is your loyalty?'

'With the winner,' she replied, and the phone went dead.

He wasn't surprised at the outcome. He knew just too well that she would always choose the winning side. But why did she have to involve Tiwari-ji in all this shit?

"Poor Tiwari-ji. Played safe his entire life and would now be fired for no fault of his. I better warn him at some point of time."

His eyes went back to the bottle of whisky. Where is she? Just one drink, he promised himself. He poured himself a Patiala to calm his nerves. But before he could take a sip, the phone rang again. This time it was the call he had been awaiting all evening.

Reputation is Important but Survival is Everything

'I think we might have made a mistake, Salil-bhai,' said Kunal.

'Which mistake are you referring to?'

'We shouldn't have sold the stock down 18 per cent. It has unnerved all the brokers. Sunny isn't the only one who called for money today. I have received similar calls from 3 other brokers, all demanding funds. Also, Mr Reddy was sounding cagey last evening.'

'That was no mistake. If I hadn't sold the stock down, then someone else would have done it. You never go against the tide of the market.'

'But how are we going to pay these brokers?'

'Who said anything about paying them? Promise them that you will and buy some time.'

'You think it's going to work? They sound quite desperate.'

'Don't worry. In a day or two, as soon as the markets stabilise, I will again pull up the stocks. All these fuckers who have sold will come scampering back. As the stock moves up, the value of the unpaid positions and collateral will increase, and none of these brokers will trouble you for funds.'

Kunal smiled.

'We have run a near perfect operation for the past three years. Now, with only three weeks remaining for the conversion of the FCCBs, I don't intend to abandon ship. Unless you are suggesting that the tide itself is turning.'

'I don't know, Bhai. No one understands the markets better than you do. All I know is that they are looking exuberant. Even my cigarette shop owner was suggesting stocks to me yesterday. I understand that you have a reputation to keep, but three weeks could be an extremely long time, should the markets turn against us.'

There was a minute of silence in the room as Salil-bhai pondered over Kunal's words. He had survived on Dalal Street because he was a cunning fox. He had a sixth sense about the markets that allowed him to see what others had missed.

Personal ego was an extremely expensive habit to maintain on Dalal Street, a habit which had led to the downfall of many czars in the past, including the biggest of them all, Harshad Mehta. The moment you broke either of the two golden rules–one, the market always knows more than you, and two, it is bigger than you–you signed your own death warrant.

Salil-bhai had a grounded personality with no false pretences about himself. He had no intentions of breaking the golden rules. Reputation was important on Dalal Street but survival was everything.

'I hear you loud and clear, Kunal,' he said. You go and buy time from these brokers. Dole out money to keep the top brass entertained, if you have to.'

'As you say, Bhai.'

'Don't worry about Reddy. He has far more to lose than I have. He will buy his stock, if that is the last thing he does.'

I am Counting on That

'Was my hypothesis correct?'

'Yes. You were right,' said Pooja. 'There is an outstanding position of almost 60 crores in those accounts, including MTM, which is not reflected in our records.'

'Do you have the collateral to cover this position?'

'Yeah, we have 100 crores of stock in addition to this position.'

'I hope you are not counting the shares of Reddy Oil & Gas as collateral.'

There was silence on the phone line.

'This collateral has little value. The stock is manipulated and the liquidity is artificial.'

'How can you be so sure?'

'Pooja, don't question my intelligence. I know stock manipulation when I see it.'

'In that case, I better speak to Jayant at once. He needs to understand the severity of the situation.'

'Also, send out margin calls to these accounts, asking them for money immediately.'

'Don't you think that the KYC on these accounts will be fudged?'

'Yeah, I am sure it is. But you need to create the records to justify your actions. We have to cover our ass.'

'What action are you proposing?'

'Chop off the positions, of course.'

'Are you crazy? Chop off 60 crores of position?'

'You have no other choice. It has to be done in one go. I suspect there are similar positions standing at various other brokerages. If word gets out, you will be left out in the cold.'

'But there will be complete mayhem.'

'Better have mayhem than a 60 crore debit which cannot be recovered.'

'Hmmm. It's time you met Jayant. I don't want to play the messenger. I will speak with him, but I need you to talk to him directly. I will set it up for noon tomorrow.'

'Sounds good. Noon it is then. Same place as before.'

Belling the Cat

Varun put the phone down and immediately called up Tiwari-ji. He wanted to ensure that Tiwari-ji was on top of everything. But Tiwari-ji was his usual self, non-committal as before.

'Why are you telling me this? I told you before, I don't want any part in it.'

'But you don't have a choice,' replied Varun. 'You're neck deep in this shit, whether you like it or not.'

'What do you mean? What the fuck have you done? Why do I get the feeling that I am being dragged into this?'

"Because you are."

'Listen, Tiwari-ji, I haven't done anything. But Sunny will fire both of us, after he has dealt with Jayant. Of that I am certain.'

'Shit! You are responsible for this.

'Please stop it, Tiwari-ji. It doesn't matter whether I am responsible or not. The fact is that our survival is interlinked. We will have to act together, if we wish to get out of this one in one piece.'

'What do you propose?'

Varun told Tiwari-ji of his discussions with Pooja, her secret investigation and its findings. After listening to him, Tiwari-ji sounded more re-assured and calm.

'I am meeting Jayant tomorrow to discuss the modalities. With this new information, Jayant should be able to manage Sunny. Is there anything you wish to add?'

'You must ensure that Sunny is out of the office when you act. Otherwise, it could create unnecessary complications.'

'Yeah, I think so, too. The only other question that still needs to be answered is, who will take over from Sunny?'

'Who will?' said Tiwari-ji, sounding edgy.

'Who else, but you.'

'Are you crazy? I can't do this.'

'Tiwari-ji, its time that you did. How much longer will you run away from responsibility? It's a great opportunity.'

'Why don't you do it?'

"Believe me, I would have, if I felt that the idea would sail through. I wouldn't be wasting my time with you."

'Are you kidding me? Let's be realistic. Till yesterday, I was part of the same coterie against whom I am conspiring today.'

'But why do you choose me? Why not one of the other relationship managers here?'

'You have the experience and understanding. You have not been corrupted by the system.'

'But I cannot do this on my own.'

"I know that only too well."

'Don't worry, I will always be by your side.'

I Need This to Happen

Salil-bhai called up Reddy first thing in the morning. He wanted to calm his nerves and instil confidence in him. Otherwise, why would Reddy buy his shares when Salil-bhai himself was reducing his position?

'How are you, Reddy sahib?'

'How are you! What do you think? I almost had a heart attack two days back,' said Reddy, not mincing words. 'I hope you remember, only three weeks are remaining for the conversion of the FCCBs.'

'Reddy sahib, I remember everything. But you must understand that Reddy Oil & Gas needs to move with the market.'

'What do you mean?'

'Reddy sahib, when a bellwether stock like Intotys can fall 6 per cent on that day, then who can prevent Reddy Oil from sinking. Think about it? If I hadn't allowed the share to fall with the market, it would have caught the attention of the market regulator.

Reddy felt a little reassured.

'I understand,' he replied. 'But yesterday the market was calm, why didn't you pull it up?'

'That's the problem, Reddy sahib. The market took us all by surprise last Monday. My liquidity position is a little tight at the moment. I will need you to buy a few lakh shares from the market to lessen my position. After that, you see how I pull this share up like a rocket.'

'But I am already neck deep in this, Salil-bhai. I don't have the money to buy a few lakh shares.'

'Don't do it yourself. I am sure, you can ask a few people in your inner circle. After all, they will be laughing all the way to the bank when the stock hits its previous highs.'

Reddy didn't reply.

'I need this to happen, Reddy sahib,' said Salil-bhai, and he disconnected the phone line.

Salil-bhai knew that the old man would do what was required. Not because he believed in his cock and bull story, but because he had no choice.

The Perfect Candidate

'Bloody hell! You have to give it to Sunny. He has balls of steel,' said Jayant. 'But I am truly shocked that he could stoop so low to make an extra buck.'

'Jayant, with due respect, it wasn't an extra buck. He was making millions every month. We were mere pawns, forced to play ball through a mix of intimidation and rewards.'

'How long was this racket running?'

'I have been aware about it for almost two years now.'

'Pooja tells me that you have some reservations about the stock collateral with us.'

'You mean Reddy Oil & Gas? It is useless.'

'But it is a stock against which funding can be provided as per the exchange.'

'Jayant, the categorisation of the exchange can be easily manipulated. All you need to do is to create liquidity, while managing the volatility. This is all part of the manipulation. If the stock is not granted a fundable status then brokers like us will not lend against it and the whole plan will fall flat.'

'Do you happen to have any evidence that similar positions stand at other brokerages?'

'I don't have any written evidence, but I am aware that similar positions are standing at another four or five brokers. I can give you the names of these brokerages if you require. But please be discreet in your enquiries. If they get suspicious and act before we do, then we will be in trouble.'

'Don't worry. I will keep it discreet.'

'Have you sent out the margin calls?'

'Yes, they were sent out in the morning. We have given them till end of day to make good their accounts. By the way, that was an intelligent suggestion from your end.'

'If I may ask, have you got any response yet?'

'No. None at all. The KYC data appears fudged.'

'Just as I had expected.'

'The rot runs deeper than I thought,' said Jayant. 'I thought it was limited to the risk and the sales departments. But if the KYC is also fudged, it implies that some people in the account opening department are also involved.'

'Yes, the entire system needs overhauling. Sunny needs to go. He cannot be allowed to continue after what he has done.'

"I know you wouldn't allow him one extra day."

There was the hint of a smile and a look of satisfaction on Jayant's face. He was going to be victorious in a long, hard fought battle. Only two days ago, the tide had been against him, and he had been fighting tooth and nail to hold on to his job. Today, the tide had turned. No one wanted Sunny to be kicked out more than he did. But Jayant reigned in his excitement.

'This is not a decision for you or me to make. The evidence will be examined and the right action will be taken by the top management.'

Varun knew too well what this meant. Sunny was on his way out.

'But if Sunny is fired, who will take over his role?'

'Not me,' said Varun. 'I am too young with neither the experience nor the acumen to lead this organisation. We need someone with experience and maturity. A person not corrupted by the system.'

'Do you have such a person in mind?'

'In fact, I do. Who better than Atul Tiwari. He checks in all the boxes. I think he will be the perfect leader to take us forward.'

"I know you love it. Tiwari-ji fits in perfectly."

Jayant knew Atul Tiwari well. They had joined the organisation together. He was smart, but would never dare to challenge authority. Exactly the credentials he wanted in someone becoming the Head of Sales and CEO.

'I couldn't agree with you more,' said Jayant smiling, further cementing his own position in the organisation. Tomorrow morning as soon as the market opens, we will chop off the positions.'

"No, No. You can't do that. It will spoil everything."

'Jayant, I suggest that you do so a little later in the day, when the stock has some liquidity. I don't think you will find the desired liquidity in the morning to chop off such a largeposition.'

'You have a point,' said Jayant. 'But it will be almost impossible to execute this operation with Sunny present in the office. He comes in late to office and I was hoping to finish it before he arrived.

'Okay, let me worry about him,' said Varun. 'I will see to it that he is busy elsewhere.

'Then it is decided,' said Jayant. 'We will take over the entire risk department at 11.30 am tomorrow and chop off the positions.'

Front Running

As soon as the meeting with Jayant ended, Varun called up Nikhil Seth.

'I have a money making proposition for you,' he said.

'Come right over,' replied Nikhil. 'I am at the farm house.'

'I would much rather meet you somewhere else,' said Varun, the events of the previous week still fresh in his mind.

'Ha-Ha! I understand,' he replied. 'But don't worry. I am a reasonable man. What happened the other night was only good business.' A little later, they sat together in his courtyard sipping margaritas.

'Nikhil, you got the wrong man. What happened with you last week was orchestrated by Sunny.'

'That's bullshit. It was Anil who called me. Not once, but several times pushing me to make the trade.'

'Yes, that's true,' replied Varun. 'It was Anil's shoulder, but someone else fired the gun. The entire bloody trade was a trap laid out by Sunny and Anil fell for it.'

Nikhil looked a bit disturbed.

'Sunny convinced Anil that the trade was a money making opportunity. Anil called you in good faith, hoping to recover your past losses. You know what happened after that.'

Nikhil's face was full of remorse as he remembered Anil crying out for forgiveness.

'But why couldn't you tell me this earlier that night?' he demanded.

'I was trembling with fear,' replied Varun. 'Too scared for my life.'

'Oh God! What have I done? I wish I had handled it differently that night.'

'What has happened cannot be undone,' said Varun. 'Anil has left the city, perhaps forever. But you can certainly do me a favour instead.'

'What?'

'Fix up a meeting with Sunny tomorrow at 11.00 am. Keep him entertained for an hour. I will do the rest.'

'Why? What will happen tomorrow?

'Tomorrow, between 11.30 am and 12.00 pm, the stock of Reddy Oil & Gas will crash. And so will the fortunes of Sunny.'

'Why should I believe you?'

'Nikhil, with due respect, do you think I am an idiot? I saw what you did to Anil with my own eyes. You think I will ever double-cross you? If you could do that to someone you like, only God knows what you will do to me?'

'That's not fair,' said Nikhil. 'But it's the truth. How big a gamble should I take?'

'As big as you want. Such opportunities come seldom.'

'What do you want in return for this favour?'

'Tomorrow evening, after you have finished counting your profits, I shall come back here and collect the documents of Anil's property.'

'Those are worth over 50 lakhs.'

'I am fully aware of that, Nikhil. I expect you to make a bigger killing tomorrow.'

Varun paused, allowing Nikhil to consider his offer.

'Ok,' said Nikhil, shaking Varun's hand vigorously. 'I owe it to him.'

'We both owe it to him,' replied Varun. 'One more thing—I hope you enjoy watching Sunny crumble, as his fortunes tumble down.'

'This is going to be priceless!' grinned Nikhil.

Let the Drama Unfold

Salil-bhai relaxed in his office. Everything was proceeding as per plan. His hard talk with Reddy the previous evening seemed to be paying dividends. The stock of Reddy Oil & Gas was trading up three per cent today, on what he presumed was buying either by Reddy himself or his inner circle.

He sold a few lakh shares early in the morning, thereby lessening his position. Now, with cash on his side, he waited for an opportune moment when market sentiment would be supportive to pull the stock up.

Brokers who sounded jittery a day earlier, were breathing a sigh of relief, seeing the price of the stock rise with volumes. He hoped that the stock would end the day up by 5-6 per cent. That should be enough to keep them off his back for a few days.

He had asked Kunal to put in buy and sell bids of a million shares each, early in the morning. As the day progressed, he planned to move up the buy bids to higher prices, triggering sale from his other accounts. The quantity of shares with him would remain the same. They would merely be transferred from one account to another. However, to an outsider, it would appear as if the share had moved up with rising volumes. This was the basic premise behind circular trading.

Strong movement of the stock with high volumes would ensure that it reflected in the charts of every technical analyst in the country. He hoped that a few of them would recommend the stock for follow through buying the next day.

He looked at his watch. It was only 11.00 am. Still an hour to go before he would start his operation.

Nikhil Seth sat in his living room with a cup of coffee. Sitting across him was Sunny with a large mug of beer. The television set was turned on in the background.

Sunny wondered why Nikhil had called him the previous evening out of the blue. As far as he could see, there was no agenda for them to meet. In fact, Nikhil looked a little lost, his mind preoccupied with something else. But then, he had a large live position in the market, cause enough for distraction.

Within 15 minutes of the market opening, Nikhil had short sold two lakh shares of Reddy Oil & Gas. He was surprised to see the firm demand for the shares. In a minute, his entire sell order of two lakh shares was absorbed by the market. Some poor bastard was aggressively buying these shares.

He had checked his position at 10.55 am. He was now losing money. Not a lot, but he was down a few lakhs. He wondered if he had been taken for a ride again. Imagine, falling for the same shit twice.

Sunny had arrived at 11.00 am sharp. They had spent the past 15 minutes exchanging pleasantries. Nikhil Seth waited in anticipation for the clock to strike 11.30 am and the action to begin.

At 11.15 am, Jayant walked into the risk department unannounced, with Pooja and a few other people from the compliance department.

'Boss! What a pleasant surprise,' exclaimed Ravinder, looking extremely suspicious.

'Boys, I need to have a quick chat with you all,' said Jayant. 'Leave your phones behind and join me in the conference room. Five minutes should do it.'

He walked into the conference room and the risk team followed.

'You two can stay behind,' said Pooja, to two new recruits who had joined only a month earlier.

Once they were all inside the conference room, Pooja quietly locked the door from outside.

The two new recruits looked at her in bewilderment.

'Don't worry, boys,' she said. 'Just do as I say and everything will be fine.'

'But what about them?'

'Oh! Don't worry about them. They are not coming out any time soon. Not until we have finished what we have come here to do.

'Now don't waste time,' she said authoritatively. 'Sit down at those terminals and do as I say. I am going to read out 12 client account numbers now. I want the two of you to split them between yourselves.'

They did as they were told, pulled out the relevant client records and placed them on their terminals awaiting further orders from Pooja.

The clock struck 11.30 am, Pooja looked at Jayant through the glass wall of the conference room. Jayant looked at her and raised his right hand. This was the signal she was waiting for.

'Boys, chop off all the positions in these accounts in front of you,' she said urgently. 'It needs to be done in one go, no remorse.'

'Are you sure about this, Ma'am? There are very large positions in these accounts.'

'Do as you are told,' she yelled. 'I know what I am doing. Don't worry.'

All Hell Breaks Loose

As the first two lakh shares hit the market, there was a sudden crash in the price of Reddy Oil & Gas. Salil-bhai immediately noticed the sudden movement and the corresponding increase in volume.

'Who the fuck is selling?' he yelled, getting up from his seat and rushing outside his cabin. By the time he reached the hall below wherein the operation of Reddy Oil & Gas was being carried out, another three lakh shares had hit the counter. The stock was now down 9 per cent from the high of the day.

'Don't bloody sit on your asses!' he yelled. 'Remove the bids! Can't you see someone is selling aggressively?'

His staff acted immediately, going into hyper drive removing bids, but their hands were not fast enough to prevent another three lakh shares being bought on the counter. The stock had now hit the 20 per cent lower circuit.

Within a few seconds there was a seller of 2.5 lakh shares at the lower circuit.

'How many shares have we bought today?' yelled Salil-bhai.

'Eight lakhs,' came back the reply.

'How many did we sell in the morning?'

'Five lakhs.'

'Shit! What is happening? Who is selling?

Not only did he hold another three lakh shares in his kitty, but the bloody stock price had crashed to the lowest level in the past many months. Was someone else playing on the counter of Reddy Oil & Gas? Did someone else possess more information than he did?

He dialled Reddy. As soon as the call connected, he heard the choicest abuses. They came in all languages, English, Hindi, Telugu reminding him of India's rich multicultural heritage. He banged the phone down. Obviously, it wasn't Reddy. He appeared to be even more distressed than him.

Unknown to him, Reddy was being hounded by his inner circle, who were calling frantically for guidance. But Reddy didn't know what to tell them. After a few minutes, he stopped taking their calls. Consequently, they panicked and dumped the shares bought in the morning adding to the ever increasing queue of shares remaining unsold at the lower circuit.

'Bhai, 10 lakh shares and counting now,' said Kunal.

'I expected that,' replied Salil-bhai. 'No more buys until I get to the bottom of this.'

'Bhai, do you want us to try and sell our own shares,' asked Kunal.

'No need. There is no way we can sell anything. We will only add to the queue of shares remaining unsold at the downward circuit. Instead, call up the brokers. They must be a worried lot.'

Kunal tried frantically to reach out to a few brokers. None of them took his calls. He looked at Salil-bhai, despair all over his face.

'None of them is taking your calls?' asked Salil-bhai. 'Even that bastard Sunny?'

'I didn't try, Sunny,' said Kunal.

'Just forget it, let me call him up. You concentrate on the others.'

Almost 15 lakh shares were now outstanding at the lower circuit.

'I need to attend this call, Nikhil,' said Sunny, walking out of the living room.

'Have you been selling Reddy Oil & Gas,' asked Salil-bhai.

'No sir,' replied Sunny. 'I can assure you, it isn't me.'

'It better not be.'

Nikhil saw the bewildered expression on Sunny's face. Perhaps, it was time for him to check on the trade. He went to his office. The stock of Reddy Oil & Gas was frozen at the 20 per cent lower circuit. He calmly bought back the two lakh shares that he had short sold in the morning.

It was time to open a beer.

He walked back into the living room, a big smile on his face and a bottle of beer in his hand.

'What happened, Sunny? You look a little worried,' he asked.

'I should go back to the office. Something has come up.'

'Come on. Have another beer with me. I just made my biggest profit,' said Nikhil.

'I am sorry, but I have to go back now,' replied Sunny.

'Hey! At least ask me about my trade,' said Nikhil.

'Of course! What did you buy?'

'Not buy, I sold. I sold Reddy Oil & Gas,' Nikhil announced with glee, now laughing uncontrollably.

'Bastard!' yelled Sunny, rushing out of the front door. He called up Ravinder, his heart pounding. 'Tell me that everything is fine.'

But Ravinder didn't answer his call. He frantically dialled him a few more times. No answer. He called up his Regional Sales Manager, who sat in the same office as Ravinder.

'Drag the son of a bitch by his ears and get him to call me back,' he said.

After a minute, the Regional Manager called back to say that the risk department was locked and he was not allowed to enter it. The entire office was crawling with people from the compliance department. Apparently, there was a meeting going on between Jayant and the risk team.

Sunny's worst fears had come true. He drove to the office to save what he could.

Time to Switch Sides

Meanwhile, in the conference room, Jayant was discussing the crash of the terminals a few days earlier with the risk team.

'There was discrepancy between our records and those of the exchange,' he said. 'Any explanations what caused this discrepancy?'

'There was no discrepancy. I can vouch for the accuracy of our records,' cried Ravinder, emboldened by the pep talk he had received from Sunny, a few days earlier.

Jayant smiled. 'There was a discrepancy a few days earlier,' he said. 'But you are right, at this moment the records are accurate. I asked Pooja to identify the discrepancy and remove it. After all, we all want the records to tally, don't we?' His smile widened.

Ravinder swung around in horror. He saw Pooja through the glass wall, giving instructions to the new recruits who were busy at work. He reached for his mobile to call up Sunny, to tell him that everything had fallen apart. But his mobile was in his office.

He desperately tried to figure out what to do next. Jayant watched his discomfort and smiled.

'I know about the 12 accounts,' he said. 'Such a clandestine operation couldn't have been possible without the active support of the risk department.'

There was silence in the room.

'Ravinder, you still want to stand by your story?' asked Jayant.

Ravinder did not answer. Sunny and Jayant were two sides of the same coin. While Sunny was driven by money, Jayant craved power. They would sacrifice anyone for their personal gain. Should he switch sides from one bastard to the other?

Almost reading his thoughts, Jayant said, 'Don't worry, I won't harm you. Holding you responsible for this mess would show me in bad light—after all you report to me.'

Ravinder's face heaved a sigh of relief. He knew that the time had come to switch sides.

Jayant also smiled. With Ravinder on his side, he could finally nail Sunny. Once Sunny had been fired, he had no intention of keeping Ravinder on. Both of them had to go. But that was for later.

The Writing on the Wall

Sunny drove at break neck speed to the office. His car screeched to a halt in front of the office building; he threw the keys towards the parking attendant and ran towards the entry gate.

The security guards stopped him.

'Who the fuck do you think you are?' he yelled in anger. 'Don't you know who I am? I own this place.'

But the security personnel stood their ground.

'Get your hands off me, you son of a bitch,' he yelled in disgust pushing one of the security guards and trying to get inside the office.

In the altercation that followed, he slapped one of them on the face. He was immediately pinned face down on the ground by half a dozen men. A large crowd gathered in no time to watch the spectacle.

He looked up the stairs and saw familiar faces staring down at him. He had been ridiculed and embarrassed, but there was no concern in their eyes and none came to his rescue. He realised that there was no point in arguing and fighting with the security personnel any more. The writing was clear on the wall. His tenure in this organisation had come to an abrupt end.

He gestured to the security guards to let him go. He slowly got to his feet and walked towards the car. Not one of his cronies came to see him off.

As he sat in the car, his mobile phone rang. It was an unknown number. Generally, he never answered unknown numbers, but today was certainly different. After all that had transpired, what could get worse for him?

'You are finished,' said Salil-bhai, and slammed the phone down.

Later that evening, Varun went to the farm house to meet Nikhil Seth. They had a drink together and Nikhil handed over the relevant documents to him.

As he got up to leave, he asked Nikhil, 'How was your meeting with Sunny?'

'He is a bad sport. Didn't even stay back for the celebration.'

It was Always You

The stock of Reddy Oil & Gas continued its downward journey for the next three weeks, settling at a fifth of its value.

Salil-bhai left Reddy sahib high and dry, exiting the counter lock, stock and barrel. Despite being able to sell his holding only after a few days of it hitting downward circuit, he ended up making a lot of money in the operation. He reminded Kunal once again that while reputation was important on Dalal Street, survival was crucial.

The brokers who had financed Salil-bhai's operations ended up with large irrecoverable debit balances.

Reddy's inner circle tried unsuccessfully to sell their holdings for a few days. However, as the stock continued to decline, they gave up hope. They held on to their stock praying that Reddy would pull off some miracle and save their asses. They knew that Reddy would sink if the FCCBs weren't converted into equity. But miracles seldom happen in real life. On the penultimate day, the FCCB holders filed for redemption of their bonds and repayment of their principal.

But Reddy didn't have the money to repay them and the matter went to court. Meanwhile, a third party emerged out of the blue which wanted to buy the bonds from the FCCB holders at a discount. Negotiations started with this party. The only thing holding back the FCCB holders from selling their bonds was their suspicion that this party was a front for Reddy himself.

Thanks to Varun, Nikhil Seth more than recovered his loss in the share of Reddy Oil & Gas. Now with money in his pocket and regained confidence, Nikhil was once again seen in the office, dabbling in the stock market.

Sunny lost his job and so did a few of his trusted lieutenants. Devika and Ravinder were amongst them. Under normal circumstances, Sunny would have found a job with another brokerage firm within weeks. Financial mercenaries like him were always in demand. But these weren't normal circumstances. He had taken on Salil-bhai, the biggest shark of his industry. He interviewed unsuccessfully at many places.

Tiwari-ji was appointed the CEO and Head of Sales on the recommendation of Jayant, who continued as the Head of Operations.

Pooja took over the responsibility of the risk department in place of Ravinder, continuing to report to Jayant. However, a few days later she resigned, shocking everyone. Jayant tried unsuccessfully to convince her to take back her resignation. But she had made up her mind.

'What happened?' Varun asked her a few days later. 'Why this sudden change of heart?'

'It wasn't sudden,' she replied. 'The decision to quit had been brewing in my mind for some time. You helped in clearing my thoughts.'

'How is that?' he asked.

'I played ball with you because we had a common objective—to clean this organisation. The incidents of the previous weeks brought out so much filth to the fore, it made me realise what I had known all along. I am a misfit here.'

'But we have cleaned it, haven't we? Why not enjoy the fruits of our labour? You have earned it.'

'Ha-Ha! You cannot cure a tumour. It can only be removed. The filth will be back again. Everything is grey here. Everyone is grey here. Whereas, I only see black and white. This organisation is not for me.'

'What about us?' he asked.

'Oh well, it was just a dream. There was never an "us". It was always about you.'

ALL'S WELL THAT ENDS WELL

I Miss His Smile Too

They sat together in a private suite at the Oberoi Hotel. The contrast between them was telling, despite the fact that Varun had made every attempt to spruce himself up. He had spent the better half of the day at a Spa, where the attendants had worked hard on him, softening his rugged face, cleaning his yellow finger nails and cracked feet. After a few hours, he had come out shining, much like a car from a car wash. Thereafter, he arrived for the meeting in the best suit he possessed. But he was no match for his host.

Punit Garg ran the second largest oil drilling company in India, as per market capitalisation. At least, that is what the statistics of the prior month suggested. However, those statistics were outdated. They had not taken into account the sudden and unexplained crash in the stock price of the largest player in the industry, Reddy Oil & Gas, wiping out 80 per cent of its market capitalisation.

The liveried waiter walked into the room carrying a bottle of Dom Perignon. No sooner had the waiter left, than Punit Garg and Varun started their business discussions.

'Please do the honours,' said Punit.

Varun had never ever opened a bottle of champagne. However, he had seen it being done in movies and at the end of cricket matches. So he shook it vigorously and prised open the cork. The champagne gushed out, spilling a quarter of the bottle on the carpet.

Punit was disappointed and amused, but didn't show it.

'Cheers to a new beginning,' said Varun, pouring a glass for Punit and for himself.

Punit took a sip of the champagne and then lifted the leather suitcase next to him, putting it down on the table between them. He slowly moved his fingers on the lock adjusting its dials and flipped open the suitcase.

Varun gasped. Inside were two hundred bundles of 1000 rupee notes. And they all belonged to him.

'Please count the money,' said Punit.

Varun pulled himself out of the trance and quickly counted the number of bundles inside the suitcase. Then he randomly pulled out one of the bundles and counted the notes in it. He looked up once he had finished counting.

'Satisfied?' asked Punit, smiling. 'The remainder after we commence the next leg.'

Varun nodded, closed the suitcase and kept it beside him on the sofa. His heart was exploding with excitement. He now had all the money in the world to fulfil every dream. And guess what? This was just the beginning.

But he remained calm on the surface, engaging in casual chatter with Punit, showing no urgency to leave.

'What will happen to Reddy?' he asked.

'Reddy is in trouble. He has gone underground. Creditors are queueing up outside his house at this very moment. I think he must be applying for anticipatory bail in some court.'

'Why is he filing for anticipatory bail?'

'Market rumour has it that during the last few weeks, Reddy was pressed for liquidity and had to raise money from informal channels. These guys are dangerous. They play dirty and can resort to any means to recover their dues.'

'I believe that the FCCB holders have also gone to court?'

'You are well informed. If it wasn't for your actions, the FCCB holders would have converted their bonds into equity. The way the stock of Reddy Oil & Gas moved up, no one could have predicted this outcome a month earlier.

'Yeah, you are right, Mr Garg. Reddy had engaged a good market operator. But then, we aren't novices either.'

'How did you pull it off, Varun? It was a master stroke.'

Varun had successfully manipulated everyone around him to achieve his goal. He was dying to tell his story to Garg, but downplayed his excitement.

'Are you sure you want to hear the long story?'

'Of course, I do. I am intrigued how you pulled it off.'

Varun happily spoke non-stop for the next twenty minutes, explaining the organisational structure, the two power centres in his office and the strong undercurrents between Sunny and Jayant.

'So, they were always at each other's throats?' asked Punit.

'Always. Sunny felt that Jayant was an unnecessary pain in the ass, never supporting his business initiatives. If there was no business, where was the need for operations?'

'Where did you stand in all this?'

'I was part of the sales organisation. Hence, my loyalties lay with them. However, to be fair to Jayant, we did exploit every possible lacuna to increase our revenues and did not necessarily play by the rules.'

'What did you do next?'

'I was managing some of the accounts of your competitor. As an insider, I had access to confidential information which was detrimental for Sunny. However, I had to wait for an opportune moment to strike.'

'Yes, I had begun to wonder if things were progressing as per plan. We had met a few months back along with Anil. Not much had transpired since then. Frankly, I had almost given up.'

'You should have had more faith, Mr Garg. Sunny was very powerful in the system. I knew that I had only one chance to act and had to wait for the opportune moment.'

'When did the right moment arrive?'

'Three weeks back when the market tanked. Reddy Oil dropped 18 per cent that day. I knew from my prior discussions with you that there were leveraged positions of Reddy Oil at other brokerages. Hence, he was vulnerable. But interestingly no margin call asking for additional funds was issued from my organisation where he had the largest position.'

'Why is that?'

'Sunny had seen to it that these accounts didn't exist in the system. So, where was the need to issue margin calls? The head of risk was on the take.'

'How did you manage it?'

'I highlighted this discrepancy to Jayant. I gave him the ammunition he needed to take on Sunny. This turned the tide. Jayant did the rest efficiently, chopping off the positions that didn't exist in the system. The rest, as you already know, is history.'

'Yes. I enjoyed seeing the stock hit downward circuit for weeks on end.'

'It had to happen. The sudden fall in the stock market took everyone by surprise and created a domino effect. Before you knew it, risk departments across organisations were scampering to chop off their positions.

'Sunny didn't try to intervene?'

'He did. But he was late. We struck when he wasn't in the office. We made sure that information did not get out till it was too late.'

'What happened to Sunny?'

'He lost his job. There has been a complete overhaul in the organisation. We have a new CEO & Head of Sales and also a new Head of Risk.'

There was silence as they both sat sipping the champagne. After a few sips, Varun asked, 'Mr Garg, coming back to our earlier discussion, why don't you take over Reddy Oil & Gas?'

Punit looked at him, a little surprised. Varun packed more than eyes could see.

'I am working on it,' he replied. 'I was the one who eventually bought the shares in bulk which prevented the stock from crashing further.'

'I had an inkling,' replied Varun. 'That's why I asked.'

'I think, unofficially, I must be holding 15 per cent of the company. I have also made an offer to the FCCB holders, to buy them out. But right now I am offering them only 50 cents on the dollar.'

'Will they agree?'

'They should. They are a worried lot. I made them aware about how long matters drag on in Indian courts. Maybe, I will also sweeten my offer a little bit.'

'Then what?'

'I shall sit down with the old man himself, Mr Reddy, and make him an offer he can't refuse.'

Garg smiled as he remembered how times had changed. Only a few years earlier, Reddy was calling the shots. He had forced a one sided deal on him. Garg had been humiliated. But he didn't have a choice as that was the only way to survive.

'On a separate note, when can we begin work on my stock?'

'Give it a month or two. Let things settle down a little. Then, we can commence work.'

'Tell me, do we need to take the new CEO & Head of Sales and Risk into confidence?'

'Of course, we will have to take them on board. It's going to cost you. But don't worry, I shall manage it all.'

Varun knew that Tiwari-ji would be a cake walk. For the first time he felt relieved that Pooja had resigned. Otherwise, this plan would have been a non-starter, as she would have never agreed to play ball. The new Head of Risk appointed in her place was more malleable. He was accommodative and thus, easily manageable. But there was no need to tell Garg about it. He could take money in their name and pocket it for himself. The only guy he had to watch out for was Jayant, who was a smart cookie.

They gulped down the last of the champagne and Varun got up to leave.

'What about Anil?'

"WTF? Why does his name keep cropping up? First it was Pooja and now Punit. It's been some time since he left. I thought everyone would have forgotten him by now."

'What about him, Mr Garg?' asked Varun.

'Where is he? Haven't seen him for a while?'

'Oh! I am sorry, I didn't tell you earlier. Anil left.'

'Left?'

'Yeah, he just packed his bags one day and left. Got into some trouble with one of his clients. I think he has returned to his village. Do you want me to find out about him?'

'No thanks. Not required. He was such a jovial, likeable character, always smiling.'

'That he was,' replied Varun. 'I miss his smile too.'

She was Always a Misfit

To,
Mr Anil Shukla
Rajwan Bazar, Meerut
Uttar Pradesh 250002

Dear Anil,

Buddy! How are you? I hope you have fully recovered from the incident of that fateful night. I came looking for you the next morning, but found the house locked.

Sorry for not reaching out earlier. I didn't have your address. I pulled it out of the office records yesterday.

I have been busy lately. Much has happened in the past month and half. For starters, Sunny is no longer in the organisation. He was kicked out unceremoniously last month. I had a big role to play in his ouster. Someone had to stand up to him after what he did to you.

Tiwari-ji has taken over as the Head of Sales. You do remember Tiwari-ji, don't you? The same guy you used to call a pussy. I guess you were right in your assessment. Even on this occasion, he tried to chicken out. But I didn't let it happen. I cornered the son of a bitch. Anyway, he has accepted the new responsibility and I am helping him out with day to day matters.

Ravinder, the Head of Risk was asked to leave, paving the way for Pooja to assume his responsibilities. However, she resigned a few days later and has left the organisation for greener pastures. She was always a misfit in this organisation. However, I must confess that if it wasn't for her, ousting Sunny would have been difficult.

Devika was also fired last month. She didn't leave me with any choice. I lost my cool when she didn't show any remorse or sympathy towards you. It was always about money for her. She left me the very day I confided in her about my plans to take on Sunny. The next morning she sang like a canary in front of him. By afternoon, all special accounts had been transferred to her.

Oh, before I forget, one last thing. I met with Nikhil Seth recently. The bastard hasn't forgiven you. His blood still boils about losing all that money. However, as a gesture of our friendship, I made him an offer that he couldn't refuse. Consequently, I have settled your debt with him. You are no longer obligated to pay him back. The lien papers of your house property are safe in my custody. In due course of time, I intend to drop these off to your house. But for now I am attaching a copy of the same.

I hope this lifts your spirits.

Your buddy,
Varun

The Son Returns Home

The pineapple cake was from Wengers. It wasn't his favourite. He preferred chocolate. But his wife would have it no other way. Pineapple was her son's favourite and that's all that mattered.

'It's my 60th birthday. At least sometimes let me have it my way,' grumbled Mr Aggarwal.

She didn't reply and continued to put the candles on the cake.

'What was the need for this big celebration,' he said. 'I don't like half of these people, and the other half I haven't spoken to in years.'

'He loves you,' she replied.

'He is only showing off. We don't even know if he will come.'

'My heart says that he will come for sure,' she replied.

'Ok. Have it your way. But if he doesn't come in another 10 minutes, I will cut the cake. I am hungry.'

Just then, Varun made a grand entrance.

'Papa, you should have more faith in people,' he said. 'I wouldn't have missed this party for the world.'

'Stop acting like a chief guest,' retorted Mr Aggarwal. 'Let's cut the cake. I can't bear these relatives any more.'

As they gathered around the cake, Varun received a call on his mobile. He looked at the name and smiled. He had been waiting for this call for over a month.

'Why did you do this? Why?' said the voice on the other end. 'I fired Anil on your recommendation.'

'It was nothing personal, Sunny,' he replied. 'It was only good business. I needed a cause to take you on and you gave me the perfect cause by firing Anil. People rally around those who fight for someone else's cause.'

'What about Devika? Was she in on this too?'

'Ha-Ha! You still haven't figured me out. I don't like sharing. Devika sold me out because she thought I was a sinking ship. I knew she would do so and therefore confided in her. You rewarded her by transferring the special accounts to her, thereby removing my name from the records. I needed this to happen before Jayant initiated the enquiry.'

He disconnected the call and joined the chorus...'Happy birthday to you'...as his father cut the pineapple cake.

The son had finally come home.

A Dip In The Share Market (Glossary)

Bear Cartel A bear in stock market parlance is an investor who is pessimistic about a particular share or the market in general. He believes that a particular share or the market is headed downward and attempts to profit from its decline, by short-selling at a higher price and buying his position back at a lower price. When bears act together in a group so as to maximise the price impact of their action, it is called a bear cartel.

Circuit Filter Circuit breakers are pre-defined values in percentage terms, which trigger an automatic check when there is a runaway move in any security or index on either direction. The values are calculated from the previous closing level of the security or the index.

Coupon Rate It is the rate of interest paid by bond issuers on the bond's face value. It is the periodic rate of interest paid by bond issuers to its purchasers.

Delivery Trade When a security is bought for investment to be sold at a later date (Nnot intraday) and its delivery is received in the depository account.

Exposure The size of investment in the market. In the context of a brokerage, it is the trading limit that is allotted to a client based on his collateral i.e. cash and stock balance.

Gap Down/Up A gap is a break between prices on a chart that occurs when the price of a stock makes a sharp move up or down with no trading occurring in between. A market is said to open gap down when its opening price is below the closing price of the previous trading day and vice versa.

In the Money An option is called in the money' when it has intrinsic value. The term is used for options on stocks or futures contracts when the price of the underlying market is at or beyond a certain level, making it possible for the option to be exercised, or converted into that underlying contract.

Intraday Exposure Extra margin (capital) given by a stock broker company for day trading to its clients. It can vary from 4 times or 10 times the client's capital or investment.

Leverage Use of borrowed capital for making investment.

Long Position A long (or long position) is the buying of a security such as a stock, commodity or currency with the expectation that the asset will rise in value.

Margin Call A broker's demand on an investor using margin to deposit additional money or securities so that the margin account is brought up to the minimum maintenance.

Mark to Market (MTM) Process of daily revaluation of a security to reflect its current market value instead of its acquisition price or book value. MTM is essential where the position has been created on borrowed funds or leverage.

Notional Profit Unrealised or paper profit arising from an incomplete trade where the asset hasn't yet been converted into cash.

Options They are contracts that grant the right, but not the obligation to buy or sell an underlying asset at a set price on or before a certain date. The right to buy is called a call option and the right to sell is a put option.

Out of Money An out of the money option has no intrinsic value. Out of the money (OTM) is term used to describe a call option with a strike price that is higher than the market price of the underlying asset, or a put option with a strike price that is lower than the market price of the underlying asset.

Outstanding Positions The amount of a security that is owned (a long position) or borrowed and then sold (a short position) by an investor.

Proprietary Trade When a trader trades securities with the firm's own money, as opposed to depositors' money, so as to make a profit for itself.

Shell Companies A company existing as a legal entity but having no significant assets, independent business operations, etc., often owned or controlled by another company and used for various, often illegal, purposes.

Short Position It is a directional trade wherein the investor sells the shares in anticipation that its price will fall.Thereafter, he buys back the shares to cover his short position.

Squared-Off To reverse an open trade. Squaring off is a trading style used by investors/traders mostly in day trading, in which a trader buys or sells a particular quantity of an asset (mostly stocks) and later in the day reverses the transaction, in the hope of earning a profit.

Strike Price The strike price (or exercise price) of an option is the fixed price at which the owner of the option can buy (in the case of a call option), or sell (in the case of a put option), the underlying security.